A GOOD NAZI?

David Canford

mad-books.com

1.21

Cover design: Mary Ann Dujardin

CHAPTER 1

It was the week after his father shot himself that Torsten first met Jozef.

The weather matched Torsten's mood, miserable. A penetrating drizzle ran down his neck, and his wet shirt now clung to his back like a leech. Low cloud hung in the valley, hiding the mountains and suffocating beauty. All seemed grey and morose.

He fought back tears as a couple of boys from his class taunted him, throwing stones at Torsten while he walked home from school. It was the words that hurt.

"Your father was a drunkard."

"A coward. Just like you."

"You're just a peasant, a peasant with holes in his shoes."

The two boys laughed.

"Hey! Leave him alone."

Torsten, who had his head down, looked up in the direction of the voice. A boy, maybe a couple of years older and taller than him and his tormentors, stood a few metres in front of him.

"What are you going to do about it?" shouted one

of the bullies.

"Kick your arses. That's what I'm going to do about it."

The bigger boy marched past Torsten and towards the others. As he grew closer, they too realised that he was significantly larger than them. They turned and ran. One tripped on the cobbles. By the time he got up again and hobbled off, he was crying like a baby.

"Thanks," said Torsten as his saviour returned.

"That's OK. I hate bullies. I'm Jozef. Jozef Messing."

"Torsten Drexler. "

They looked each other up and down. Torsten was a typical German. His hair the colour of straw, his eyes a pale blue. Jozef, however, was different to the normal resident with eyes of deep brown and hair as black as coal. His complexion was almost Mediterranean.

"They were right. You do have holes in your shoes."

Torsten said nothing. He was embarrassed. His mother had been promising to get him some new ones for ages, but he knew they didn't have enough money. His parents used to shout at each other when he and his brother and sister were in bed. Their lack of money often featured in those arguments.

"Come with me. My father's a shoemaker."

Jozef led Torsten to the bridge over the river separating Partenkirchen from Garmisch, two adjacent towns in the Bavarian Alps. Torsten's shoes began squelching from the water which had seeped into them. He tried walking on tip toes and then his heels to disguise the noise but to no avail. Torsten had to almost run to keep up with Jozef. He hoped they would soon get there. One sole had now completely detached itself from the front of his shoe, forcing him to assume the gait of a penguin.

Jozef led him to a wooden building on the edge of town. A small metal sign with the word "Schuhmacher" swung in the light breeze. In the small window, whose glass had a long crack running diagonally across it, finely crafted shoes were arranged on two sloping shelves. They looked out of place at this rather downmarket establishment.

Inside, the air smelled strongly of leather. A bald man with thick, round glasses was sitting on a stool, bent over his work bench sewing a shoe by candlelight. Other half finished shoes stood in a line, waiting their turn. The scene reminded Torsten of 'The Elves and the Shoemaker', a story which his mother used to read to him when he was younger from the tattered old book of the Brothers Grimm Fairy Tales she had been given as a girl. In the dim light Torsten also noticed several skis in various stages of preparation were lined against the wall.

"Papa, my friend here needs his shoes fixing. Could you help him, please?"

The man got up but he remained stooped, his shoulders rounded from a life of rarely looking up

from his table.
"Let me look at them."
His words were uttered slowly as though he must be permanently weary and was about to yawn at any moment. Torsten removed the boots and gave them to him.
"Why don't you take your friend…er-"
"Torsten."
"Your friend, Torsten, upstairs and get your mother to give him something to eat while I work on them."
Jozef led him up what was more a ladder than a staircase.
"There's a step missing half way up. Watch out for it."
Torsten had to stretch his leg to reach the next one. Upstairs, there was even less light than below. In the shadows, Torsten could see a woman wearing a headscarf and stirring a pan on a stove.
"Ruth, Miriam. Go."
Two teenage girls quickly disappeared behind a sheet that hung across the room before Torsten got the opportunity for anything more than a brief glance. The mother said nothing. She cut a piece of bread from a loaf on the table and handed it to Torsten before returning to her cooking.
"Danke schön."
"Where do you live?" asked Jozef.
"In Partenkirchen, near the main street."
"That's probably why I've never seen you before. I don't go there often. Only when Papa wants me to

deliver shoes to his customers. Do you ski?"
"No."
A couple of boys Torsten knew did. It made him envious. However, as his family struggled to afford the basics, anything that wasn't essential was out of the question.
"I could teach you. Papa makes skis and sells them to the ski shop in town. I have my own pair which he made, and I could borrow another pair from our shop. The owner of the ski shop says he makes the finest skis in all of Germany.
"He also says that I have the makings of a champion. The snow will be further down the mountains soon. There's skiing on the summit already but I have no money for the cable car. Did you know there's a train too now. It opened this summer. Maybe that will be cheaper, I don't know."
Jozef's face lit up as he talked of skiing. His enthusiasm was infectious, lifting Torsten's spirits.
"Boys, come down. These are beyond repair," said Herr Messing once they had climbed down the ladder.
"Thank you for trying, sir," said Torsten.
"I have a nice pair of boots that should fit you."
Torsten received the proffered footwear hesitantly as though they were some precious artefact in a museum which he shouldn't be handling.
"Don't be shy. Go ahead, try them on."
The boy sat down on the floor and pulled them on. He had never owned anything like these. They were of the highest quality, the leather so soft and

supple. As he tied the laces, he was already wishing that he could keep them.

"Walk around in them. How do they feel?"

"Wonderful, but I can't take them. I can't pay you."

"That doesn't matter. You can come and help me after school sometimes. I'm falling behind with my orders, and Jozef needs to spend more time doing his school work."

"Of course. I could come Wednesdays."

"Good. I will teach you how to make the best shoes. Then when your boots finally wear out, you will be able to make your own. What do you think?"

"That sounds perfect, thank you."

CHAPTER 2

Torsten felt as if he was floating on air as he half ran and half skipped back home.

"My, what's got into you?" said his mother when he flung open the door. Though she always tried to sound chirpy if Torsten had ever bothered to pay enough attention he might have noticed that it was all an act, put on for the sake of her children. Under her eyes which had once sparkled, the skin was as grey as her hair was starting to become. Life's tribulations had beaten her down and worn her out. Black, which as a widow she was now condemned to wear, added to her pallor.

"I have new shoes, Mutti. Look." Torsten pointed triumphantly at his feet.

"Well, they are splendid I admit, but where on earth did you get them from?" His mother's forehead creased with a frown. "You know we can't afford them. You didn't steal them, did you? You must take them back to wherever you got them from straightaway."

"I was given them. I met a boy whose father's a shoemaker in Garmisch. I'm going to help there after school to repay him."

"You better not be lying to me, or you'll be feeling that up there on your backside."

His mother looked up at the stick which she kept on top of the cupboard. She only had to touch it for Torsten and his siblings to stop misbehaving.

"I'm not lying, Mutti. I swear I'm not."

"I'll show no mercy if I find out that you are. At least you'll have something decent on your feet for your father's burial tomorrow."

His joy evaporated as he remembered. Torsten glanced at the corner of the room, their only downstairs room, where a coffin had been laid upon a chest of drawers. That, a cupboard, the dining table and chairs were the sum of the furniture which they possessed apart from their beds.

The coffin was longer than the chest and finely balanced on it. Their mother hadn't been able to afford to have the coffin stored at the undertakers. The children were currently forbidden from playing indoors in case they should inadvertently knock it off.

It disturbed Torsten to think that they were sleeping under the same roof as a dead person. What if his father had already become a ghost and floated around the house at night? He might not be a friendly ghost, if such a thing existed. In life, he had been irritable with a fiery temper.

"I don't want to go. It's so shameful," protested Franz, who at thirteen was two years older than Torsten. "Even the Church won't give him a funeral."

"Well, shame on them," said Frau Drexler. "He fought for his country. The Great War destroyed him and people should show some compassion. You are going whether you like it or not. We shall all honour his memory."

That night, in the bed which he shared with his brother, Torsten couldn't sleep. He had struggled to sleep since coming home last week and finding his father.

The others had been out and Torsten was the first back. His father had been sitting in a chair, his wooden crutches lying on the floor beside him. The end of a rifle was still in his mouth, the bottom of it wedged between his inner thighs. The man's eyes were wide open as if he had been taken by surprise. It wasn't until Torsten had got closer he'd noticed that part of the top of his father's head was missing.

Torsten had immediately ran out into the street screaming. He'd run straight into the arms of his mother who had just arrived home with his sister, Ingrid. Frau Müller, who lived next door, had taken the children in until his mother had cleaned blood from the wall and floor. She didn't come to collect them until a coffin had arrived and Rudolf Drexler was inside it and the lid had been nailed down.

Torsten remembered how his father used to refuse to go out, how he'd heard him crying when his children were in bed, shouting at other times. He would say he was so ashamed that he didn't work, so ashamed that his wife had to take in washing and go clean other people's houses to put food on the table.

"I wish you had known your father when I married him," said their mother that awful evening of discovery. "He was so handsome in his uniform, so full of life. Losing his legs broke him. I know that your memories are of a man who always seemed angry and resentful but that wasn't the real him. This country betrayed him, gave him no support. Our so called Weimar Republic.

"Did I ever tell you how when you were little children a loaf of bread cost a billion old Marks? People would use wheelbarrows to carry their money. And even now things aren't much better. There aren't enough jobs. We need a saviour, but I don't know where we're going to find one."

Noticing the three pairs of eyes before her brimming with tears, she regretted her words.

"I'm sorry, my dear children. I shouldn't have worried you so. Things will be all right. I'll be able to take in a lodger now. Ingrid, you can share my bed. And Franz and Torsten, you can move out of your room and sleep in Ingrid's bed on the other side of the curtain which divides my room. That way we'll have a spare room to rent out, and I can find more work now that I don't have your father to look after."

"Ingrid's bed's tiny and Torsten wriggles like a worm," complained Franz.

"Well, you'll have to try sleeping head to toe and if

that's no better, learn to put up with it. None of us can have all we want in this life. We have to make do and be grateful for what we do have."

On the day of the burial, the sun shone in a cloudless cerulean sky. It was one of those October days that could make a heart soar. The trees had turned a defiant yellow and burnt orange in a dying blaze of glory. The mountain peaks were a brilliant white as they wore their new headdress of snow like icing on a cake, softening their jagged outlines.

The entire family resented that nature had chosen to dazzle on today of all days. They had hoped for a repeat of yesterday's mournful grey that obscured all colours, for rain that would have kept people inside. It seemed almost as if the entire town had turned out to gawk from their doorways.

The siblings and their mother kept their heads down as they walked slowly, balancing the coffin on a shoulder and steadying it with one hand. At the rear were Frau Drexler and Franz, and at the front Torsten and Ingrid, the coffin sloping down towards them. Torsten could feel wood splinters digging into his hand. It was a cheap coffin, not sanded down, nor had the wood been varnished. A confirmation for all to see of how poor the family were.

They could sense others' eyes staring at them. Were they judging? Did they feel any sympathy for a man who had committed what the Catholic

Church considered to be one of the very gravest of sins, taking his own life? The priest had refused point blank to countenance any church funeral or burial on sacred ground.

Suicide was also a crime. The punishment would fall on the family left behind. His small disability pension would end.

It would be a good ten minute walk to the farmer's field. His son had been killed in the war and he had readily agreed Herr Drexler could be laid to rest on his land.

Rudolf Drexler hadn't been a large man. However, even with no legs beneath the knees and thin from a life of often being hungry, his weight and that of the coffin dug into their shoulders. It made them ache, an ache that intensified with every few steps. But they couldn't put it down, not in front of so many watching eyes.

Ingrid stumbled on the cobbles. Biting her lip to deflect her attention from the pain in her shoulder, she regained her balance.

"Let me take it for you."

She moved gratefully aside. Torsten twisted his neck to look at the new pallbearer. In his free hand he carried a pair of ladies' shoes, doubtless another delivery he had been tasked to undertake. It was Jozef.

His gallantry encouraged others. Soon the Drexlers had all been relieved of their burden and were able to walk behind. Frau Drexler was pleased to see men removing their hats. Others joined the family cortege. By the time they reached the field, the crowd was quite sizeable. After the burial, many came to offer their condolences to her.

"He was a hero. He fought for this land."

"He was worth more than all those useless politicians in Berlin put together."

"If Hitler ever becomes Chancellor, your poor husband's service will be recognised."

"Yes, Herr Schmidt is right. We need someone to stand up for us, make us proud again to be Germans."

Frau Drexler sniffed to maintain her composure, touched by the unexpected outpouring of support. Torsten stood with her and his siblings, fidgeting and longing for it all to be over. Once the last in the line of adults waiting to express a concern, something which they'd never done when his father lived, had spoken to his mother, Torsten looked around for Jozef. He had already gone.

CHAPTER 3

The following Wednesday, it seemed to Torsten that class would never end. All he could think of was getting to Herr Messing's workshop. He wanted to learn to make shoes like him. Then maybe he would be able to make his mother a pair as well as some for Ingrid and Franz. He gazed out of the window, thinking how impressed with him they would be.

"Drexler." A gruff voice snapped him out of his daydreaming and brought him back to the present. "Stand up, boy."

Torsten stood beside his desk. A stocky man advanced towards him. Herr Gruber, their new teacher. He had started that week replacing Fraulein Abels who had now married and could no longer continue with her job. Whereas she had radiated compassion and serenity, Gruber appeared to function on anger and scowls. Despite a plump, round face that could have conveyed Bavarian good humour, this man showed no such inclination.

"What was my question to the class, Drexler?"

"I...I'm sorry, sir, I didn't catch it."

"No, of course you didn't. You were staring out of the window. Come with me."

Grabbing Torsten by the ear, Gruber marched him to the front of the class.

"Maybe this will remind you to pay attention."

Gruber took the stick lying on his desk and struck it hard several times on the back of Torsten's legs in the gap between his short trousers and long socks. Torsten resisted the urge to cry out. He was determined not to give Gruber that satisfaction. His legs stinging with pain, Torsten walked back to his desk. Several of the boys smirked at each other, enjoying the spectacle.

Torsten's legs were still hurting when he reached the shoemaker's across the river in Garmisch, but he forced himself to put that out of his mind. Unlike school, his new lessons were ones that he was eager to receive.

"Ah, so you came. Jozef is out on a delivery. Today you can watch and next week I'll let you have a go."

Torsten observed with fascination the dexterity of Herr Messing as he cut out leather for the soles and uppers, the intricacy of his stitching, and the care which he took in nailing on the soles. Torsten's hands were almost trembling the following week when he was given some leather to cut.

"Don't look so worried. This is an off cut I had left over. It won't matter if you make a mistake."

After a couple of attempts Torsten improved markedly, his nerves no longer getting the better

of him as Herr Messing peered over his shoulder.
The bell above the door rang as Jozef entered.
"How's our new helper doing?"
"I think he's going to take to it like a duck to water."
Torsten beamed with pride. It wasn't often that he received praise.
"That's great. The snow's moving down towards the valley floor. Are you free Sunday morning to try some skiing? We have spare skis you can borrow."
"Really? Yes, I'd love that."
Since the Church had refused to bury his father, Torsten's mother no longer required the children to attend mass, leaving him free to enjoy his Sundays and do exactly as he wished.
Torsten arrived early at their pre-arranged meeting spot, eager for his first attempt. In the distance he spotted Jozef, distinguished by the long, thin wooden skis which he was carrying, one pair on each shoulder.
"Are you ready for this?" said Jozef as he arrived.
"Absolutely."
"Take these."
Torsten struggled awkwardly as the two skis he had been given slipped around on his shoulder, separating and pointing at different angles.
"You must equalise the weight. Position them so that the mid point is on your shoulder and grip them firmly with your hand. That way they will stay together. It's going to be a long walk."

It was, but Torsten didn't object. Happily, he trudged uphill through the snow behind his hero. When they had gained some altitude, Jozef showed him how to use the leather bindings to keep his boots in place.

"Right, time to have a go."

Though they hadn't climbed that high, Torsten swallowed hard and felt his heart thumping in his ribcage when he looked down the slope. It hadn't seemed that steep as they had walked up it. The houses below looked to him like toy ones now.

"Do what I do and you'll be fine. Just remember to turn often."

Jozef set off. Torsten stood, frozen with fear.

"Come on," Jozef called from below.

Torsten cautiously shuffled his skis until they were no longer at ninety degrees to the slope and were pointing ever so slightly downhill. They began to move slowly under him. The motion alarmed him. He increased the angle, planning to make a turn exactly as Jozef had but that didn't happen.

Torsten soon found himself with the skis pointing vertically down the slope, accelerating quickly. He was like a runaway train, unable to apply a brake. He whizzed passed Jozef who was shouting at him to turn. Not knowing what else to do, Torsten threw himself onto the snow and slid prostrate down the slope.

In a few seconds, Jozef had caught up. Seeing Torsten was only shaken up and not hurt, he put his hands on his hips and laughed.

"That was probably a bit ambitious. Let's try further down where the incline is negligible."

Jozef spent the rest of the morning patiently tutoring Torsten until he had acquired an element of control. As they hiked back to town, Torsten asked the question which had been on his mind since their first meeting.

"Why are you being so kind to me, Jozef? You treat me better than my brother does."

"Maybe because I don't have my own brother any longer. He died."

"Oh."

"It was about this time last year. They told us he must have drowned while playing by the river, but I don't believe it was an accident. The local bullies used to chase him. I think they pushed him in, or he fell in trying to get away from them. My parents went to the police to complain about them, but they were told to go away. One of the bullies is the son of the police chief. They just want to cover it up. When I saw you being attacked, something inside me made me react. It brought it all back to me. Isaac was only your age. I wasn't there to protect him."

They walked the rest of the way in silence.

"Did you want to try again next week?" asked Jozef as they parted.

"Yes please."

Torsten grinned all the way home. Never had he thought that he would get the chance to ski. He had considered it was only a sport for the monied classes, like those who arrived here in winter from Berlin and Munich to engage in the latest fashionable pastime of downhill skiing. Torsten would now be luckier than even they were. They could only come for a few days each year but he lived here. He would be able to ski all season long. What with that and learning to make shoes, his life had never been more enjoyable.

CHAPTER 4

Early Monday evening the family were sitting around the table when there was a sharp knock on the door.

"Who could that be?" asked Ingrid.

"I expect it'll be the lodger. I'm glad you're all here to greet him. We must make him feel welcome. He will be paying us a good rent." Helga Drexler opened the door. "Welcome, do come in. Let me introduce you to my children."

They stood up from the table, curious to meet the person who would be living with them. As their mother moved aside to reveal their guest, Torsten's heart sank. It was his teacher. Gruber shook their hands, pushing the corners of his lips upwards into a forced smile.

"Ah, Torsten. We know each other already. He is a pupil in my class."

"A good one, I hope," said his mother.

"We have had the occasional difference of opinion, but I think he has turned the corner. Isn't that right?"

Torsten didn't respond. Everything in his life had only so recently changed out of all recognition for the better. Couldn't that feeling of good fortune have lasted a little while longer? Of all the people his mother could have let a room to, why did that despicable man have to be the one.

"Children, you may go outside and play while Herr Gruber eats his dinner and gets settled in."

They wandered along the street. Their house was at the bottom, farthest from the centre. It looked practically derelict, not having been properly maintained in years.

As they moved up the street, the chalets grew larger. Many were painted white with dark wooden shutters and had wooden balconies. Some sported elaborate frescoes of Bavarian rural life or a religious scene. They would have looked attractive in any setting, but with their Alpine background the scene was as charming as a pastoral painting. It was a place of good order and tranquility, insulated from the troubles which beset so much of the world beyond.

"You'll be teacher's pet now," teased Franz.

"No, I won't. I can't stand him."

"Well, you better get used to him. I doubt he'll be leaving any time soon."

"What was that armband that he was wearing? Red with a white circle in the middle and a black symbol?" asked Ingrid.

"He must be a member of the National Socialist German Worker's Party," said Franz.

"The what?"

"The Nazis. They're led by some Austrian guy

called Adolf Hitler. Apparently they got a fifth of the vote in last year's election and seats in the Reichstag for the first time. But what they stand for I don't know. You should ask him."

"It can't be anything nice if he's a member," muttered Torsten.

"Oh you're such a baby, sulking because you got into trouble for misbehaving. You have your head in the clouds these days. Just because you begged for some new shoes and found a friend who let's you use his skis."

"That's a lie. I didn't beg. Take it back."

"I most certainly won't."

Torsten swung his fists at Franz.

"How dare you, you little pipsqueak."

Soon they were rolling around on the ground wrestling.

"Stop it!" demanded Ingrid.

"I hate you!" Torsten wiped his sleeve across his bloody nose and ran back the way they had come.

"He's such an idiot."

"And you're so mean," countered Ingrid. "I think you're jealous that he's learning to ski."

"No, I'm not. It's so stupid, sliding down a hill on pieces of wood. When I grow up, I'm going to join the army and do something useful for our country."

It wasn't long before Torsten became accustomed to having Herr Gruber in the house. He ignored him as much as he could by retreating upstairs or going outside, although at weekends that was more difficult as the family ate their meals with him. It seemed that having him lodge might even be an advantage. At school Gruber rarely scolded him any longer, albeit Torsten took care not to give him reason to.

On Sunday, Torsten met up again with Jozef and this time he stayed standing.

"I have some good news. Herr Brandt, the ski shop owner, has agreed to coach me. And he says that he's willing to let you come along as well to see how you do. Isn't that amazing?"

"Are you joking?"

"Of course not. Be at the ski shop this time next week."

Torsten awoke late and almost didn't get there in time.

"Come on in." Herr Brandt beckoned to Torsten, who was tentatively looking through the window. There were several other boys in the shop as well as Jozef, all eager and clearly delighted to have been asked to attend.

"You must be Torsten Drexler."

"Yes, sir."

Herr Brandt was thin and athletic looking, which wasn't surprising given that he was well known as the area's pre-eminent skier.

"Welcome boys to our inaugural get together. I'm looking to form a junior downhill ski team. My goal is to develop those of you who show the aptitude and dedication to become excellent skiers with a view to being picked by our national team.

For the very best, there could be the chance of Olympic glory. The German Imperial Commission for Physical Exercise has successfully lobbied to host the 1936 Olympics. The summer games will be in Berlin. They haven't said yet if they want to stage the winter ones also, but I expect that they will, and they could even be right here in our beloved home town."

A collective sound of surprise and excitement erupted.

"Though the winter games which will take place next year in Lake Placid in the State of New York don't feature Alpine skiing, I'm confident that by 1936 it will be a recognised sport. So are you ready for hard work, heartache, and of course lots of fun?"

A roared yes of agreement filled the room.

CHAPTER 5

"I'm very pleased with your progress, Torsten, and thankful for your help. I think you have probably earned your boots by now. I shall have to start paying you," said Herr Messing as they worked together in his workshop.

"That isn't necessary. I'm just grateful to acquire a new skill. Though perhaps if it was acceptable to you, I could make some shoes for my mother for Christmas."

"Yes, of course. When can she come in to be measured?"

"I wanted it to be a surprise."

"But to have the perfect shoe, you must take careful measurements of the feet."

"I could measure her existing shoes when she's asleep."

"Did she have her feet measured for those?"

"No, she bought them second hand."

"That's no good." Herr Messing shook his head firmly. "But I have an idea. You can pretend that I have asked you to practice feet measurement before I let you loose on my customers. I can lend you a tape measure. I shall write down what you need to do, and draw you a diagram. Make sure you double check it all. We want them to fit perfectly."

That same evening, Torsten persuaded his mother that she should let him practice on her.

"Ah, it's so nice to take these old boots off. They do rub so. Herr Gruber is out at some meeting or other tonight so I shall warm my feet by the fire when you're done."

Torsten got down on his knees and began measuring. His mother squirmed.

"Ooh, that tickles."

"You must keep still, Mutti."

"I will try."

"Well, you must. It's hard to see down here on the floor. It's so dark with only the firelight."

Clutching her hands together, Frau Drexler fought to stay still. She flung her head back and shut her eyes, trying hard to ignore the feeling. But it took several attempts. She just couldn't stop writhing and giggling for long enough. Still, it had the whole family laughing too, something which they hadn't done much of in a long while.

"You can relax, I'm finished now."

"Thank the Lord."

"I hope your first real customer isn't that ticklish," said Ingrid.

"Maybe you're just lousy at it," said Franz.

"Franz, stop that right now. Your brother's doing very well. Maybe you should find something to occupy yourself other than chopping wood for the fire. I appreciate it, but you need to find an interest."

Franz grunted. "Hmm. I'm off to bed."

Later that week, Ingrid plucked up courage to question Herr Gruber as they all ate together.

"Franz says that armband you wear means you're a Nazi. What's one of those?"

"Ingrid, don't be so impertinent. It's none of our business. I do apologise for the intrusion, Herr Gruber."

"No need, Frau Drexler. I'm glad that you asked, my dear. We believe in saving our nation. The way our government has behaved is a national shame, a disgrace. Look at how your father was treated after he gave so much for this country. Our leaders have betrayed us. They conspired with our enemies.

"After they capitulated in the Great War, they allowed Germany to be brought to its knees. In the Treaty of Versailles, Germany had its colonies stolen. Land in the east of the country was handed to Poland and in the west to France. They control the size of our army and forbid us to have an air force. How can we call ourselves a nation when others tell us what we can do?

"Jews and international bankers lend our government money on extortionate terms. Our leader, Adolf Hitler, would end all that. Give us back our sense of national identity and pride. Create jobs for the unemployed. Make Germany great again."

Herr Gruber brought his fist down on the table, swept up in his own rhetoric.

"A few years ago, he led an uprising in Munich to free us. They accused him of treason and threw him in jail. But he's too strong to keep down. I believe that we will win the next election, and then it will be a wonderful time to be a German."

Ingrid shrank back into her chair, wishing that she'd never asked. The way Herr Gruber's voice had become increasingly loud and strident scared her.

Torsten hadn't paid attention. Adult talk was so boring. All he cared about was skiing and shoemaking in that order.

Franz, however, absorbed what he had heard. He felt lost and confused without a male role model, something which his father hadn't been able to provide. When he was older, he could be part of this plan for making Germany great again. Then his family would appreciate him, and the other boys at school would look up to him. He would no longer be ignored by everyone.

"Well, let's hope Herr Hitler wins then. What are your plans for Christmas?" said Helga Drexler trying to change the subject.

"I'll be going to visit family in Munich for a few days."

"That will be nice."

And don't bother coming back, thought Torsten.

True to his word, Herr Brandt, his ski instructor was a hard taskmaster. Even though at times it seemed that every one of Torsten's muscles ached, he thrived on the discipline required and the exhilaration of the sport. A couple of the boys had already dropped out, but Torsten was determined not to. He and Jozef became the star pupils in the ski team, although he knew Jozef was better than him.

In early December, snow fell down in the town itself. Thick and fluffy, it rested on the roofs and covered the streets with a soft carpet.

On the evening of 5 December, the night before St Nicholas' Day, the family stood outside their door watching local men dressed in fur and wearing horns and devilish masks go from door to door. Known as Krampus, these half goat, half demon figures visit houses in Bavaria to frighten children into good behaviour. Spotting the Drexler children, two came over.

"Who is the eldest child?"

"Franz," answered Torsten, gleefully indicating his brother.

"And does he misbehave?"

"Oh yes," laughed Frau Drexler.

Before Franz could make a move, they had grabbed him by the legs and had him hanging upside down.

"Shall we?"

"Yes," cried out the rest of the family in unison.

Taking their cue, the men unceremoniously planted his head in the snow before letting him fall. Even Franz had to see the funny side of it and was grinning as he got up, dusting the snow off himself.

With money from the rent received, Frau Drexler wanted to make this Christmas season special. It had always been the hardest time of year. It hurt to see the thinly disguised disappointment on those young faces. The only gifts which she and her husband had been able to give were gingerbread men she had cooked, and crudely carved wooden figures that her husband made from the large branch from a fir tree which she had found the forest floor and dragged home behind her.

This Christmas Eve, Frau Drexler sent the boys to collect a Christmas tree that she had reserved. She allowed her offspring to decorate it with some brightly painted wooden ornaments she had recently purchased. There were soldiers in blue jackets and red trousers, angels, a snowman and a Saint Nicholas in green. She had also made gingerbread stars which she gave them to hang. Hoping that with their backs turned she wouldn't notice, their mother scolded them each time they nibbled on one.

A gingerbread house that Ingrid had helped her make, took pride of place on the table next to the advent wreath of four red candles flickering in a circle of small pine branches and cones. Mixing with the smell of the pine was that of cloves and cinnamon from the Glühwein warming on the stove. Never had their house looked cosier or smelled more inviting. Their most difficult year was ending on a high note.

"I wish Papa was still here to share all this with

us."

Frau Drexler reached out her hand across the table to touch her daughter's.

"I know, Ingrid. So do I, but I'm sure he's looking down on us and smiling. He would want us to celebrate and not be sad at Christmas time."

"If he hadn't been so selfish and killed himself without thinking about the rest of us, he would still have been here."

"Franz, I know you're hurting like we all are, but let's try and remember the good things, not the bad. Tonight we have a special dinner to enjoy. First, I have gifts for you all."

All three of them exchanged looks of unbridled joy as their mother unlocked the cupboard in the corner of the room. She handed them parcels tied with string and wrapped in pages of the Völkischer Beobachter, the Nazi party newspaper which Herr Gruber had delivered to the house.

For Ingrid, there was a Bavarian dirndl, and for Franz a new coat and trousers. There was a new hat, gloves, and a coat for Torsten.

"They will keep you warm while skiing. It will get much colder soon," said his mother.

After trying them on, Torsten hugged her.

"They're perfect, Mutti, thank you. I also have something for you. Stay there while I go upstairs."

He came back down, his arms behind him. "Shut your eyes and hold out your hands."

Seated in a dining chair, his mother did as asked.

"You can open your eyes now."

"Gott im Himmel. These are beautiful." The delight on Helga Drexler's face shone as brightly as the leather of the black boots. "Did you make them?"

"With a lot of help from Herr Messing. Try them on."

"I feel like Cinderella putting on a glass slipper." She did them up and stood.

"Walk around in them. What are they like?"

"Marvellous. They are so comfortable. They fit like a glove. Come here, mein Liebchen, and let Mutti give you a kiss."

"You make Ingrid and me look bad," complained Franz.

"You mustn't feel like that. I didn't expect anything from any of you. The boots are lovely, however the most important thing is that we are all here together. We must always love and care for each other, and protect one another. The real magic of Christmas is not presents, it's the love we give and receive. Now let me finish cooking, and then we can eat."

The meal was better than any of the children could ever remember. They had goose, sausage and apple stuffing, red cabbage and dumplings, and for dessert a Stollen which their mother had made.

"How did we afford all that?" asked Ingrid as she and her mother washed up afterwards. "I can't imagine Herr Gruber pays us enough rent to cover it."

"Well, it helped but, yes, it wasn't enough. Herr

Gruber spoke to his contacts in the Nazi Party and they sent me some money in recognition of your father's service for our country. Wasn't that nice of them?"

CHAPTER 6

In March, the ski team undertook their first trip to the summit of the Zugspitze, Germany's highest mountain. Sitting on the Austrian border, and at three thousand metres high, this colossus towers above the two towns below. The thrill of the ride up in the cable car was only the beginning of a day that Torsten would never forget.

At the top, the view was breathtaking. The snow sparkled with brilliance as though it were encrusted with millions of diamonds. On the west summit, a tall gilded iron cross stood from which hung numerous icicles, giving it a bizarre other worldly appearance as if marking the border to some fantasy land. Below them, were glaciers and on the horizon, mountain peaks seemingly without end.

Favoured by good weather, they could see for a considerable distance. Herr Brandt explained that not only were those imposing mountains they could see in Austria but also in Switzerland, and even the Dolomites in Italy. For once, the boys were absolutely quiet, completely awed by the magnificence of their surroundings.

Herr Brandt led them on an adrenaline-fuelled ride down the mountain. His pupils followed his lines, effortlessly carving through fresh snow like a troupe of ballet dancers making identical movements. It was grace personified.

All too soon for them, spring arrived and the snow retreated ever higher until just a few stubborn pockets remained. As he lay in bed early one morning, Torsten could hear the timeless jangling of bells as a farmer drove his cattle up the street towards mountain pastures, a sure sign that winter was well and truly over. The doldrums descended on the boy like a damp mist. Winter was now without doubt his favourite season and the next one seemed so very far away.

Torsten's downbeat mood didn't last however. Spring and summer brought new adventures for the children lucky enough to live in this special part of the world. White was replaced by a fresh and vibrant green. The grass looked so delicious, it almost made you want to taste it. Wild flowers bloomed in profusion. Trickles became streams, and the river a raging torrent of white and turquoise from the snowmelt.

Come June, Torsten and Jozef spent much of their free time swimming in the lake and warming themselves in the sunshine as they lay in the soft grass afterwards.

The adults seemed preoccupied by the forthcoming election. At least it kept Herr Gruber out of the house most evenings which suited Torsten. Franz

had been recruited as a helper, posting leaflets through doors. One July day when Torsten returned home from a day by the lakeside, the two of them were laughing and joking together.
"We've done it. We are now the largest party in the Reichstag."
Franz appeared genuinely excited also. Torsten couldn't understand why. His brother was such a weird person. Who cared about such matters?
"I'm convinced there'll be another election soon. No one has enough seats to form a government and next time we shall prevail. But that isn't the only good news, is it?"
Herr Gruber looked at their mother. Helga Drexler smiled at him, and went to stand by his side. If Torsten had noticed such things, he would have got a clue of what she was about to tell them from the fact that his mother was no longer wearing black. Instead, she had on a green dress which she hadn't worn since his father's death.
"Wolfgang and I have become good friends, more than friends in fact. He has asked me to marry him and I have accepted, and you will have a father again."
"Congratulations." Franz went to his mother, embracing her before enthusiastically shaking the hand of his soon to be stepfather. Ingrid hugged her mother and let Gruber give her a peck on the cheek.
"Will I get to be a bridesmaid?"
"We're not having a church wedding," said Gruber.

"Religion is holding the new Germany back. We shall marry in the town hall, but you shall have a beautiful new outfit to wear. I promise."

Torsten's eyes filled with tears. He turned and ran upstairs. When his mother went to go after him, Gruber put out his arm to stop her.

"Leave him be. The boy will come round in due course. It's a big surprise for him, for all of them."

Torsten didn't enjoy the wedding, though his siblings appeared to. Franz was genuinely pleased about the match. Ingrid was more cautious but today her eyes shone with pleasure at finally getting to wear her new dress of pale blue which had come all the way from one of Munich's department stores. She had also been allowed to put on some makeup for the very first time. Ingrid swelled with pride as she overheard guests complimenting her mother.

"Your daughter is so beautiful, just like you."

"I do so adore the flowers you are both wearing in your hair."

"Wolfgang is a lucky man to marry into such a lovely family."

"Stop scowling like a spoiled brat. This is Mutti's day, not yours," Franz reprimanded his brother.

Torsten recognised few of the guests who attended the wedding. They and their wives were mainly acquaintances of Gruber. Afterwards, they all went for a meal in a restaurant. There was much drinking and good cheer. However, that cheer didn't extend to Torsten.

Gruber got up to make a speech. Torsten didn't pay attention until he sensed that everyone was looking at him. They had already stood to toast the couple. As Torsten scrambled to his feet, the others raised their right arms.

"Heil Hitler," they chorused.

Torsten wondered what on earth that had to do with the marriage. Why had his mother done this to him? They had been happy as they were. They didn't need Gruber.

He consoled himself with the thought that it was now late September and not long until he would be able to ski once more. Herr Brandt was talking of them travelling to Austria and Switzerland this winter to compete.

And they did. Torsten had never left the town before, not even caught the train to Munich. Jozef did incredibly well, always in the top three. Torsten came third on a couple of occasions. On his return, his mother proudly hung his bronze medals on the wall.

"Wait until you hear what your brother has done," said Gruber, who didn't seem to regard third place as a reason to congratulate his stepson.

"What's that?"

"I've joined the Hitler Youth," announced Franz.

"You should too," said Gruber.

"Why would I want to do that?"

"Because it will make you a man, a true patriot."

"I'm too busy skiing and making shoes."

"Huh, such pastimes are frivolous. If you want to

serve the Reich like Franz here, you must forget those."

"But I don't want to. I don't care about politics."

"The boys are different, Wolfgang. I think we should let them each pursue their own interests," said Helga Gruber.

In bed that night, Franz prattled on excitedly.

"Now the Führer has become Chancellor after banning the Communists for burning down our Parliament building, there will be no more false claims about our leader or our party, and every young person will want to join the Hitler Youth."

It has never been established for certain who was to blame for the arson attack. Many believe that the fire of February 1933 was started by the Nazis to give them an excuse to take over as they hadn't won enough votes in the second election of 1932 the previous November to control the Reichstag. Their vote had in fact declined from the July election.

"Father says our nation will rise like a Phoenix from the ashes. We will become the masters of Europe."

Torsten grimaced at the way Franz used that term. He would never acknowledge that ogre as his father.

Torsten invited his family to watch the end of season slalom race. Ingrid and his mother came. His stepfather claimed a prior engagement, and Franz was allegedly too busy with the Hitler Youth to attend.

"How talented you are. The way you ski past all those poles and so close to them, yet so fast," enthused his mother as he came over to them afterwards.
"Not as talented as the winner. I would like to introduce you to my friend, Jozef."
The young man with him bowed his head.
"Delighted to make your acquaintance, Frau Gruber."
"Ah Jozef, I'm delighted to meet you too. I have heard so much about you. You must thank your father for teaching Torsten how to make shoes."
"And this is my sister, Ingrid."
Ingrid felt herself blush. Jozef was so handsome and strong looking.
And wasn't there something familiar about him? That was it. He was the one who had relieved her of the coffin that awful day eighteen months ago. He was taller and more manly looking now, but it was definitely him. Those dark eyes which mesmerised. How could she forget those.
"Jozef and I must go find Herr Brandt for the debriefing. I'll see you later."
They walked off.
"What a charming young man Jozef seems, don't you think?"
"Oh..erm...yes, I suppose so," answered Ingrid.
The junior ski team stood in a circle around their coach.
"Congratulations. That was an outstanding display. You have all progressed so much this winter.

I'm proud of each and everyone of you. Especially you, Jozef, our victor."

The others clapped while Jozef looked down and twisted his feet from side to side in the snow, embarrassed from being singled out.

"Before you go boys, I have some wonderful news to share with you. I have been told the German government, which has exercised its option to hold the winter games, will shortly be informing the International Olympic Committee that Garmisch-Partenkirchen, as they propose to call the venue, is to be the chosen location, and for the first time Alpine skiing will feature."

Torsten looked at Jozef.

"I bet you'll be on the team."

"You too."

"Maybe, but you definitely deserve it."

Come April there was even more unexpected news.

CHAPTER 7

"What's happening about dinner? I'm starving."
On arriving home from school, Torsten was disappointed to see that his mother hadn't even begun to cook.
"We're going out."
"Out. Why?"
"To celebrate."
"Celebrate what?"
Torsten didn't like the sound of that. He had become wary of surprises ever since the day his mother had announced she was marrying Gruber.
"You will find out soon enough. Until then you'll just have to be patient."
Gruber was unusually jovial when he arrived back from school.
"Ingrid and Torsten, I want you to put on your Sunday best. And you Franz, you know what to wear, don't you?"
As they walked through the town, recently installed Nazi flags, long and thin, fluttered in the wind. Franz was dressed in black shorts and a tan shirt with a rolled black neckerchief, the uniform of the Hitler Youth. Like Herr Gruber next to

whom he proudly strutted, he wore the Nazi armband. Frau Gruber strolled behind, with Torsten and Ingrid bringing up the rear.

"What's going on?" he whispered to his sister.

"I don't know," replied Ingrid.

They arrived at one of the grandest houses in town. It was more like a villa than a chalet. A fence surrounded the front garden and a gigantic swastika flag hung from a balcony above the front door. Wolfgang Gruber led them through the gate, and then turned around to look at them.

"What do you think of your new home?"

"New home?" asked his stepchildren, their faces rankled with confusion.

Their mother moved to be next to her husband, her hands clasped together and her face all smiles. "The Party has appointed your father as head of the district, and this is where we shall be living."

Franz and Ingrid displayed looks of delight. Torsten's demeanour was ambiguous as he processed the news, wondering what effect it would have on his life.

"Heil Hitler," shouted Franz, clicking his heels together and raising his arm.

The others responded in kind, save for Torsten.

"Come, let's go meet our housekeeper, Frau Brenner. And then you can see your bedrooms. You will each have your own," said Gruber.

That finally brought a broad grin to Torsten's face. The place was a palace compared to what they had been used to. The children ran upstairs to inspect their rooms, after being greeted by Frau Brenner,. Her black clothes and severe countenance made Torsten think she must be married to the child catcher, who at one time his mother used to threaten would come and take them away if they didn't behave.

All were on a high when they came back down to the drawing room while the housekeeper put the finishing touches to dinner. There were opulent sofas and armchairs. No longer would hard, straight-backed dining chairs be their only choice of seating. Also, there was the miracle of light at the flick of a switch. Their inside existence would cease to be one of shadows and corners as dark as the interior of a confessional.

A large portrait of the Führer hung above the fireplace, dominating the room. Torsten thought the man's penetrating eyes were watching him. It was like that scary film that they had seen at the cinema last week where the murderer had a hiding place behind the wall, able to look through the holes in the painting where the eyes should have been.

"Well, do you like it?" asked their mother

"Like it? It's fantastic," said Ingrid.

"I'm so proud to have you as my father."

"And I to have you as a son, Franz."

"Will you carry on teaching?"

"No, from tomorrow I shall be performing my new duties."

That was music to Torsten's ears. Although he

had moved class last September, it was still awkward to have Gruber at the school. His classmates teased him about it.

The family's financial fortunes had suddenly changed out of all recognition. As wife of the area's most important Nazi, Helga Gruber was expected to dress accordingly.

"Torsten, do you think you could ask Herr Messing to make me some more shoes," she asked him one afternoon as they were sitting in the drawing room. "Shoes like these. No more solid Hausfrau boots for me this summer." She tore the page from the magazine which she was reading and gave it to him. "I'll need three pairs. One in each design. In brown, green and red. Of course I will pay whatever they cost to make. I don't expect any favours."

As Torsten walked from Partenkirchen to Garmisch he didn't pay any attention to the signs which had recently gone up. Jews not wanted, they said.

Once again, he spent most of that summer school holiday out at Lake Riessersee with Jozef. One day, Ingrid asked if she could come along. Torsten reluctantly agreed on condition that she brought a picnic and promised not to embarrass him in front of his best friend.

It was a lovely July day. Small cotton wool clouds peppered the sky, rarely blocking out the hot sun. Jozef, who was already there, jumped to his feet when he saw Ingrid. Torsten ran ahead to reach him first.

"I'm sorry, but I couldn't stop her coming. At least I got her to bring us a huge picnic."

"There's nothing to be sorry about. Ah, Ingrid, how nice to see you again."

She was wearing her blond hair up with a plaited braid around her head, and was dressed in a traditional green Bavarian dirndl.

"You too. I hope you're hungry."

She opened the wicker basket which she had brought, and laid out a red and white checked cloth on the grass before getting out the plates and food.

"I have bread which I made this morning and some salami I bought from the butcher's on the way here. And cheese, strawberries and cherries."

"It all looks delicious, but I'm afraid I don't eat pork."

"Oh, sorry, I wasn't thinking."

"Let's go swimming," said Torsten to Jozef after they had eaten.

"Later maybe."

"Well, I'm going now."

Torsten disrobed down to his shorts and walked off feeling irritated. He knew that he should never have brought his sister. When he returned they were still talking to each other.

"We're going for a stroll. Did you want to come along?" asked Jozef.

"Can't you see I'm soaking wet."

"We'll leave you be then so you can dry off in the

sun. We won't be long."

Torsten was still grumpy when they returned.

"I must go back now," said Ingrid. "Mutti wants me to help get things ready for the veterans' reception we're having later this afternoon. Auf wiedersehen, Jozef."

"I hope she didn't bore you to death," said Torsten once she was out of earshot.

"Not in the least. Why did you never tell me how delightful your sister is?"

"She's just a girl, like all the others. Now will you come for a swim?"

CHAPTER 8

"Can you take these shoes to Frau Gruber's for me. You know where they live now, don't you? In that huge house at the top of the street. Tell her that there's no charge. Her husband's a powerful man. I'd like to keep on the right side of him," said Herr Messing.

"He's a Nazi, how can you possibly do that?"

"Just about the whole town are committed Nazis. But maybe things will change for the better. Now that they have power, they don't have to demonise us any more to get elected."

Jozef couldn't help but feel trepidation as he walked up the garden path. It was a beautiful house they now lived in. Red geraniums cascaded over the flower boxes beneath their windows. If only it wasn't all spoiled by that ugly flag. It was so sinister. It shouted out bigotry and hatred for anyone who was different.

A man opened the door in response to his knock.

"Herr Gruber?"

"Yes, what do you want?"

"I have your wife's shoes, sir. My father says there's no charge."

"And you are?"

"Messing, Jozef Messing."

"Are you Jewish?"

"Yes."

"We don't buy from Jews. Take your shoes and get off my property."

He slammed the door in Jozef's face. For a moment, Jozef remained there, in shock. Though later he asked himself why he should have been taken aback. Many long term customers had already stopped dealing with his father.

Wandering down the street, he heard someone call his name. He turned around. It was Ingrid hurrying towards him.

"I'm sorry, Jozef, about my stepfather. I was looking out of the window. I saw what happened."

"That's OK. It's not your fault."

He went to go, but hesitated.

"Would you like to go for a walk tomorrow evening? I could meet you down by the forest on the edge of town."

"Yes. I'd like that. But perhaps it would be better if you didn't mention it to Torsten."

"No, I won't. Say at seven?"

Ingrid nodded.

Inside the house, Gruber stormed into the living room to confront his wife.

"What the hell did you think you were doing ordering shoes from a bunch of filthy Jews?"

"He makes wonderful shoes and for a very reasonable price."

"I don't care if he makes the best shoes in all of Germany. This family is to have nothing to do with Jews. Didn't you think about how that would reflect on me if it got out that you bought your shoes from a Yid? These people are the enemy."

"I'm sorry, I didn't think it mattered so much."

"Well, next time maybe the back of my hand will make you think." Torsten, who was leaning over the upstairs bannister, could hear their conversation. How he loathed that pig who called himself their father. "Said his name was Messing, Jozef Messing. Is that the family Torsten has been helping?" There was silence. "Answer me woman or you will feel the back of my hand right now."

"Yes."

"I shall forbid him to have anything further to do with them. He can join the Hitler Youth instead. And Ingrid will join the German Maidens so she can learn about being a good wife and mother."

"But-"

"No buts. There shall be no further discussion on the matter."

Torsten shrank back out of sight as Gruber left the room.

"The bastard says that I can no longer come help in your shop, and that I must join the Hitler Youth if I want to stay in the ski team," Torsten told Jozef when they met by the lake the next day. "But it won't effect our friendship. I won't let it."

"My father will be sorry to lose you. The whole world seems to have gone crazy. At least it's just a few months until the ski season starts again. I don't know what I'd do if I didn't have that to look forward to."

"Me too."

Torsten attended his first Hitler Youth meeting a few days later, determined not to like it. Most of all he resented that he had to go with his brother, who was already well ensconced in the local branch. Other boys greeted him and ignored Torsten.

Franz and his colleagues put on a show for the newcomers. Banging side-drums and blowing bugles, they confidently marched back and forth. Then, having changed into white vests and gym shorts, they put on a sporting display. There was running and hurdling, aerobatics on parallel bars and javelin throwing.

Torsten couldn't help but be impressed. He recognised many of the boys. Many of them who not so long ago had looked pale and lethargic, appeared transformed from poor specimens into athletic young men.

The man in charge lectured the new arrivals, lauding Adolf Hitler, who he told them, had made all this possible. The Hitler Youth would make these boys into extraordinary men, he assured them.

What caught Torsten's attention above all was being promised a special dagger marked "Blood and Honour" once certain tests had been passed. One of the daggers was passed amongst the new recruits so they could all handle it and be consumed

with the desire to qualify for one.
The bottom two thirds of the hilt was black and in the centre was a diamond shape in red and white containing the swastika. The top third was silver coloured, like the blade itself on which were engraved the words "Blut und Ehre!"

CHAPTER 9

1933 turned into 1934 and winter came to an end. Construction of the 'Olympic House' began in Garmisch at the foot of the ski jump that was also being erected. Hitler was credited for the area's new found prosperity. Newsreels at the local theatre showed how there were jobs for every man who wanted one. Jobs for everyone, save for the Jews.

Despite his statement of intent the previous summer, Torsten didn't see Jozef once the ski season ended. He had found a new interest. A best friend had been good, but now he was part of something far bigger. There was marching, bayonet practice, grenade throwing and assault courses to occupy him. It was much more exciting than hanging around by the lake.

For the first time, he almost began to appreciate having Gruber as his stepfather. Other boys had been impressed when they found out the connection, and now treated him with respect. No longer was he the odd one out, the loner with just one friend. The taunts that the only friend he could find was a Jew became a thing of the past.

Torsten was taught the Nazi dogma, learned that "We belong to the Führer, body and soul." And before the next snow fell he could recite by heart those speeches of Hitler that he was required to learn, such as:

"The weak must be chiselled away. I want young men and women who can suffer pain. A young German must be as swift as a greyhound, as tough as leather, and as hard as Krupps steel."

Torsten had earned his dagger. How proud he felt upon receiving it up on a podium, in front of his mother and the great and good from the locality. Enthusiastically, he gave the Nazi salute.

Now he understood what Gruber and others had been saying all along. Germany was threatened both from without and within. The nation had to stand together to protect itself. Jews and communists wanted to destroy it. If the Führer hadn't taken control, they most certainly would have, selling it off to the same enemies who they had collaborated with during the Great War to engineer Germany's defeat.

Not that he believed that all Jews were evil. There were bound to be some who were decent like Jozef and his father. They didn't cause any trouble. But perhaps they were a rarity, the exception rather than the rule.

Torsten sang along with the rest of his colleagues to *Das Judenblut vom Messer spitzt, geht's uns nochmal so gut (The Jews' blood spurting from the knife makes us feel especially good).*

By now, the Hitler Youth was the only permitted youth organisation. All others such as the Boy Scouts and church youth groups had been shut down. The Nazi leadership understood that by indoctrinating the young, they would create a source of obedient, fanatical adults to fight for Germany when the time came. Encouraged to denounce their parents and teachers, those amongst the older generation who didn't approve of Hitler kept their mouths firmly shut.

At home, only Ingrid lacked the enthusiasm of the rest of her family. She frequently missed meetings of the German Maidens and argued constantly with her mother.

"Ingrid's sixteen now. We should begin thinking about introducing her to the son of a good family," said Gruber to his wife as the family sat eating dinner one evening, talking as if his stepdaughter wasn't present.

"Wouldn't that be nice?" said Helga Gruber to her daughter.

"No, I'm too young."

"Nonsense. I was only sixteen when I first met your father."

"Maybe she already has a secret sweetheart," teased Franz.

"Do you, Ingrid? There's no shame in that if he's from a respectable family."

"No, mother. I don't. May I be excused? I have a headache."

"All right. Go upstairs and lie down. I'll come

check on you later."

"That girl worries me, Helga," said Gruber. "She's too headstrong. You need to take control of the situation. It's your duty as a mother, a mother of the Third Reich."

"I'll have a word with her. She'll come round, I'm sure."

When winter came again, Torsten returned to the ski team. He and Jozef exchanged brief nods. The Nazi armband Torsten wore spoke instead. Jozef kept himself to himself, turning up just before practice and leaving as soon as it ended.

A few weeks into the season, Herr Brandt gave them the news which they had long hoped for.

"The German League of the Reich for Physical Exercise will be visiting us next week. They are looking for suitable members for the German Olympic ski team. It's the culmination of what you've all been training for these past few years. I'm confident that our standards are amongst the highest, and that there are amongst you those who deserve to be picked. I know you'll all try your utmost. What greater honour can there be than representing your country when the eyes of the whole world will be on us."

"Heil Hitler," shouted some of the young men.

Herr Brandt did the same but without much conviction. After practice, he called Jozef over and dismissed the others.

"Jozef, you're our best skier by far. You should be selected."

"I'm a Jew. They won't want me."
"They want Olympic glory, that's what they want. Can I suggest you wear a Nazi armband next week."
"I can't do that."
"Jozef, listen to me and listen carefully. You and your family could be in danger. Getting on the Olympic team, winning a medal, these things will protect your family, could get you a passport out of here if need be. Think about it, please."
Brandt smiled to see that Jozef had taken his advice the following week, even if Jozef did look more uncomfortable than usual. He introduced the group to the two officials sent by Berlin before a bus took them to the cable car for the ride up the Zugspitze. The three metre high golden cross which stood on the summit had been covered with the Nazi flag suffocating it's Christian message.
The boys skied all morning under the watchful gaze of the officials from the German League. They remained impassive throughout giving no indication of who, if anyone, they might choose. On returning to the ski shop in town, Jozef was asked to stay behind.
"Jozef, Herr Meister and Herr Vogel here were extremely impressed by your performance."
"Yes, Jozef. You are a superb skier."
"Thank you, sir. It's really thanks to Herr Brandt's coaching."
"Indeed, he has done an excellent job. We would

like to offer you a place in the national team. They will be coming here next season before the Olympics, so you would be able to train without having to travel anywhere. What do you say?"

"I'd be honoured."

"Good. We'll be in touch with Herr Brandt, and he'll inform you of the detailed arrangements in due course."

"See, what did I tell you," said Herr Brandt after they had departed. "All you need to do is make a few compromises."

CHAPTER 10

Torsten felt downhearted as he trudged home through the snow. Why had only Jozef been asked to stay behind? It could only mean one thing. Yes, he was the best skier of all of them, but other than him no one could match Torsten. Why hadn't he been offered a place too? Did they even know that Jozef was Jewish?

When Torsten reached the house and tried to sneak quietly upstairs, his mother called him into the living room.

"Torsten, come here. I should like to introduce you to Herr and Frau Drucker, and their son Hans."

A young man about his brother's age, who he recognised from the Hitler Youth, stood up to shake his hand as did his father. Torsten dutifully inclined his head forwards in front of Frau Drucker who remained seated.

Ingrid was sitting quietly next to her mother, her eyes looking down at the floor. Her bearing indicated that she would rather be anywhere than here at this moment.

"Torsten is a great skier. Today scouts came down from Berlin to watch them. They are looking for those suitable to be in our Olympic team."

"You must be so proud, Frau Gruber," said Frau Drucker.

"I am. As I am of all my children. They are such a credit to Wolfgang and I. How did it go, Torsten?"

"Well. I think. They said Herr Brandt would be hearing from them soon. I must go change. Nice to have met you all."

As he went up to his room, Torsten wondered if his stepfather would allow him to stay in the ski team any longer, now that he hadn't been selected. Gruber had never once come to watch him, thought that it wasn't important. He wouldn't be happy with his stepson spending time going all over the Alps again this winter and missing meetings of the Hitler Youth, not if Torsten wasn't going to be in the Olympics.

Though what could Torsten do, other than keep the news to himself? Yet that would only buy him a week or two at most. His stepfather was bound to find out sooner or later. It was less than a week afterwards that Gruber got the news. He burst into Torsten's bedroom.

"I've just seen Herr Brandt."

"Oh." Torsten sought not to betray the fact that he already knew.

"Well done, my boy."

Torsten was too astonished to speak.

"You've been offered a place on the team. The Olympic ski team. I told him you'd be over later to accept."

"Really?"

"Yes, really. This is such an honour. Doubtless the Führer will attend the games and want to meet the German team. Do you realise just how fortunate you are? The other boys would give anything to be in your position."

Gruber ruffled the boy's hair. Torsten tried not to wince.

"Well, don't just stand there. Get over to the ski shop."

Torsten ran all the way.

"My stepfather just told me," he said breathlessly as he entered.

"Yes, congratulations. I assume you accept their offer?" said Herr Brandt.

"Of course. Did anyone else get chosen?"

"No, it's just you. Apparently, they found out about Jozef being Jewish so they withdrew their offer to him."

"You look unhappy about that."

"We all know he was the best skier." Brandt regretted his choice of words almost as soon as he'd uttered them. The young were such zealots these days. Only last week a teacher had been dismissed for mentioning in class that Jews had fought for Germany in the last war. "But that's not the point. We need those who are loyal to the Reich, and I'm sure you will do well. I'm looking forward to helping you win."

1934 became 1935 and winter became spring. By order from Berlin, the two towns became one under the name Garmisch-Partenkirchen much to the chagrin of the locals. Each town had always been proud of its separateness.

Franz celebrated his eighteenth birthday and being accepted into the Schutzstaffel, better known as the SS. Frau Brenner prepared a special meal to mark the occasion and Franz wore his new grey uniform at the table.

"You look so handsome. My eldest son, all grown up. I can't believe it. You make me feel old."

"You make us very proud, Franz. In a few years, you too can join him, Torsten. After you've won Olympic gold first," said Gruber.

"I'll try my very best, but there will be some stiff competition. It is the Olympics after all."

"Maybe, but you have an advantage. None of them will know these mountains like you do, and the entire home crowd will be routing for you. The Führer himself even."

Ingrid suddenly put her hand up to her mouth and rushed from the room.

"What's wrong with her?" asked her stepfather

"I'll go see in a little while. Probably something's she's eaten."

After the meal when Torsten had gone up to his room, he heard his mother's voice coming from his sister's room which was next to his. She sounded agitated. He put his ear to the wall, straining to hear.

"What do you mean you're pregnant? You and Hans will have to get married immediately before it shows."

"I don't want to marry him."

"Well, you should have thought about that before you got yourself into this mess."

"It's not his."

"Not his? Well, just whose is it?"

There was no reply.

"You shall answer me, Ingrid,"

Ingrid said something but she spoke too softly for Torsten to hear.

CHAPTER 11

His mother's voice was louder and he heard her.
"Jozef. Jozef Messing? That Jewish boy. Ingrid, how could you?! If it had been Hans' baby that would have been bad enough, but this is disgraceful. Don't you know they passed a law making it a crime to have intimate relations with a Jew. I am ashamed of you, so ashamed of you. I'll need to talk to your father."
"No, please don't, please."
"Does Jozef know?"
"No."
"Good. You will stay in your room and not breathe a word about this to a soul."
Torsten heard his mother turning the key in the door and descend the stairs.
"Wolfgang, may we have a word in your study?"
The following morning at breakfast Ingrid wasn't there. His mother was pale and her eyes puffy.
"Is Ingrid still unwell, Mutti?" asked Torsten.
"No, she had to leave bright and early."
"Leave?"
"Yes, to catch the train. Your father and I have been worried about her for some time. I thought

that perhaps with Hans she would find happiness, but it hasn't worked out. I fear there's no future for her here. Your father and I decided it would benefit her to go away for a while. He knows a good family in Berlin who she can stay with."

"For how long?"

"A few months."

"Why didn't you mention this last night?"

"We only finally decided yesterday, and we didn't want to take the focus away from Franz. It was his night. I must get on. I'll see you after school."

Torsten hid the anger which he now felt towards Jozef. His mother mustn't know that he'd been eavesdropping. Jozef had taken advantage of his sister. That was a terrible thing to do. If it wouldn't have risked getting Ingrid into trouble, he would have reported Jozef for sleeping with his sister to the authorities.

Torsten loved Ingrid, not that he'd ever tell her that. When his mother had remarried, only Ingrid had understood his pain. They'd had long discussions about it. She'd been kind to him. Now they'd sent her away. He would miss her, miss her so very much.

Ingrid didn't even return home for Christmas.

"She is so happy in Berlin, she asked if we would mind terribly if she didn't come back. I shall miss her of course, but your father and I are just pleased that things are working out well for her," explained their mother.

Torsten was soon so busy training with the German national ski team that there wasn't time to think about anything else. He forgot about Ingrid. He was worried. The standard was high and the others had a definite edge on him. Torsten would need to go even faster.

In practice, he pushed himself harder. He would need to cut down on the number of turns. And he did, until one day he lost control. Almost buried in the snow when his long tumble down the slope ended, Torsten went to get up. A searing pain shot up his left leg as he put his weight on it. His leg gave way under him and he fell back down into the snow.

At the hospital he cried into his pillow when the doctor had gone. A broken leg. Torsten was out of the Olympics. His dreams of representing Germany, winning a medal and being not only a local but a national hero, were finished.

Now he wouldn't get to meet the Führer. In a country where posters portrayed the disabled as a burden on hard working Germans, a young man on crutches wasn't going to be in the line up with his family to meet Adolf Hitler.

Come the opening day of the games in February, he could hear the cheering even though his bedroom window was closed. Leaning on his crutches, he got up and looked out. A crowd several rows deep stood either side of the street, oblivious to the heavy snow falling. In the lead up to the games there had been an unusual lack of snow causing much consternation. Almost as if the Führer had magical powers it was now arriving in prodigious quantities.

Above the heads and through the raised arms he could just glimpse the man himself, standing up in the official car. Overcome with emotion, Torsten flung open his window and shouted "Heil Hitler" as loudly as he could.

When he thought about it later, he liked to think that it was him Hitler had smiled at, though he couldn't be sure. As the man passed, he turned his head until it was opposite Torsten, as if he was looking straight at him.

Later that day Franz burst into his room, his face flushed with excitement.

"I wish you could have been there. I shall never forget today as long as I live. Father, mother and I were presented to the Führer when he got out of the car at the entrance to the stadium. He congratulated father in helping organise his welcome and kissed mother on the hand.

"We were then allowed to take our seats in the stadium. You should have heard the roar when he entered. It was deafening. Forty thousand people cheering our leader. The athletes paraded in front of him, led by our own team. All saluted our great leader, giving the Nazi salute. Though some say the way in which the British and Americans saluted with their arms out sideways is the Olympic salute.

"I overheard someone telling father that afterwards the Führer went to confront the American ice hockey team in the locker rooms for their disrespect. He told them Germany would beat them on the ice tomorrow. Their spokesman apparently had the audacity to say that not only would Germany not do so, but that the United States will always defeat Germany. In my opinion, they should be thrown out of the games and sent home. Anyway, I'll see you later. I'm going back out to join the celebrations."

After his brother had left, Torsten threw his crutches across the room in frustration.

The USA did beat the German team. Britain took the gold that year, Canada silver and the USA bronze. Though Germany took Gold and Silver in the Alpine skiing event, and came second in the overall medals table behind Norway.

Torsten never took to the slopes again. However, the discipline drilled into him in the Hitler Youth soon focussed his mind on subordinating his regrets to the needs of the Fatherland. Hitler's boldness and success electrified him and his peers. Every few months they received news of his latest achievements.

Less than a month after the Winter Olympics had ended, Hitler sent troops into the Rhineland in contravention of the treaty ending the First World War, which had required the region to be kept as a demilitarised zone. In the summer, Germany topped the medals table at the Berlin summer Olympics. In March 1938, German troops annexed Austria and a few months later Sudetenland, the

German speaking parts of Czechoslovakia.
The rest of the world looked on and did nothing. In failing to respond militarily to him sending troops into the Rhineland, Britain and France had squandered the best chance they had to thwart Hitler before he became too powerful to remove.
One November evening in 1938, Gruber flung open the door to Torsten's bedroom.
"Get dressed and meet me and Franz downstairs."
"Why?"
"Just do as I say and be quick about it."

CHAPTER 12

Torsten followed Gruber and Franz out of the house and down the street towards a large group of men and youths. Several carried lit torches which gave a warm glow to the night. Torsten was puzzled. It was too soon for the traditional Christmas parades.

He recognised colleagues from the Hitler Youth and adults who played a prominent role locally in the Party. Gruber pushed his way into the centre of the gathering.

"Some of you may have heard of the attack by a Polish Jew on one of our diplomats in Paris the other day. I am sad to say that he has today died. It is our patriotic duty to avenge this despicable act. It's time to drive out the last Jews in our midst. Like the sewer rats they are, let's force them out of their hiding places."

Shouts of agreement answered him. Gruber led the mob through the town.

By now there weren't many Jews left in the area. There was an old lady who hadn't moved. Torsten remembered her from when he was young. She always had a smile for the children, a threat to no one.

When they reached her house, one of the gang threw a rock at her window. It sounded like breaking crystal as it shattered. Others broke down the door.

Soon they had dragged out the terrified woman. Protected only by her nightdress, she looked like a small creature surrounded by a pack of hungry predators, standing there alone and vulnerable. For a moment nothing happened. Then a man moved forward and shoved her so forcefully that she fell to the ground.

"You better be gone by sunrise," he shouted as the group moved on, leaving her lying there.

This was repeated at the homes of the other Jews in Partenkirchen.

"OK, we've taught them a lesson they won't forget," said Gruber. "I think we're finished for the night."

"What about over in Garmisch," called out a voice at the back. "The Messings still have their shop."

"Yes, let's," agreed another.

When they got there Torsten wished he could slink away. But he couldn't, it would be noticed.

First they smashed the shop window and pulled out the shoes, stamping on them, and then setting them alight.

"They're not coming out. Let's set the place on fire!" shouted one of the men.

A torch was thrown through the door which they'd forced open, then another. The wood soon caught alight, illuminating Herr Messing's workshop. His tools and partly finished shoes lay on the work table, the very table which Torsten had once sat at and worked under the man's patient supervision.

The shutters upstairs opened. Torsten could see Herr Messing looking down at them. The crowd booed. Torsten drew further back, hoping that Jozef's father wouldn't recognise him amongst the mob. Herr Messing soon closed the shutters.

Torsten waited for the family to come down. They didn't.

The flames had taken hold, dancing like evil spirits which were no longer invisible. Soon there would be no way through them. Torsten pushed through the crowd and moved forward towards the door.

"What are you doing?" Gruber grabbed him by the arm.

"You said that we needed to drive them out. Let's go drag them out. They'll die in there."

"It's their choice. They could have come out. Move back."

Torsten could see that all faces were fixed on him. There was nothing he could do. If he broke ranks, he would be seen as a traitor.

He retreated, watching in horrified silence while others cheered as the building became engulfed in fire and pieces of burning wood broke away and fell to the ground. The heat on his face from the fire was many times stronger than the summer sun. Torsten fought to swallow the vomit rising in the back of his throat.

There was an ominous sound of creaking, like the timbers of an old ship in a storm straining to breaking point. The building began to collapse. Some at the front were struck by burning planks. They screamed out in fright as others dragged them away, throwing their coats on them to put out the flames.

Soon it was all over. Nothing remained of the family home but a pyre of death with occasional flames leaping skyward as though in a bid to break free, knowing they too would soon die.

"Our task here is complete," announced Gruber. "A good night's work by all. The Führer will be proud of us."

Torsten was at the rear as they marched back to the bridge and into Partenkirchen. He didn't join in the anti-semitic songs they were singing.

"You need to toughen up lad," Gruber told him once the group had split up and they were walking towards the house. "There'll be worse things when you are called upon to fight. Just remember, it's us or them. If you're weak, you will die."

Torsten couldn't sleep that night. He couldn't stop thinking about what they had done. It had been easy marching around the parade ground chanting slogans, easy to bayonet dummies. The reality of killing people was completely different and deeply traumatising. He felt such guilt, such shame. Torsten tried to convince himself that the family had got out somehow. Through a back door maybe. But he couldn't remember ever having seen one.

They had murdered a whole family. Herr Messing who had been so kind to him, his wife, their two daughters. And Jozef. Ingrid had never returned home after what Jozef had done to her, but he didn't deserve to die.

Maybe others shared his concerns about what had happened, but he dare not mention them. A word out of place could have you imprisoned, or worse. The state demanded complete and unquestioning obedience.

All over Germany that night similar attacks occurred. Known as Kristallnacht, the night of breaking glass, it was the beginning of the end for the Jewish population.

A couple of nights later, Torsten was out on patrol with another Hitler Youth member, not that a patrol was really necessary. It was highly unlikely that any enemy agents would be present here in rural Bavaria, even though government propaganda had the whole country believing that nowhere was safe.

Complaining of stomach cramps, the other young man left Torsten on the edge of town. It was a pleasant night, cold but clear. The outline of the mountains framed a sky full of stars. He was in no great hurry to go back home. Torsten now dreaded going to bed. Lying there alone in the dark, his mind would be consumed yet again with thoughts

of that awful night.
Torsten wandered further. He shone his torch randomly. A fox ran across the shaft of light and disappeared into a nearby barn.
Curious to get a closer look, Torsten followed the animal. Inside, he moved the light back and forth in an arc. The cattle shifted uneasily in the shadows, their breathing heavy.
He spotted a movement, a shape disappearing behind the cattle. It was too big to be the fox.
Torsten withdrew his dagger from its sheath and pushed past the cows.

CHAPTER 13

A man stood in the corner. Unkempt and unshaven, he squinted in the bright light.

"Jozef?"

The man didn't answer. He put his right hand above his eyes, trying to see who it was shining the torch at him. Torsten lowered the beam to stop it blinding him.

"It's me, Torsten. What are you doing here? Where's your family?"

"They died in the fire. The house was burned down with them still in it." Jozef's voice trembled with barely controlled emotion, cracking like breaking ice. Torsten looked down at the straw on the floor in shame. "But I expect you already know that. You and your Nazi friends. Father had heard there might be trouble so he sent me off to the forest to hide our valuables. I wish I hadn't gone. I wish I'd stayed with them. When I came back there was nothing left. Nothing. Have you any idea what it's like to find your entire family has been murdered?"

Torsten was at a loss for words.

"You can take me in. I don't care what happens to

me. Kill me now if you want. Go on. Be a hero for getting rid of another Jew. Or are you a coward like the rest of them? Picking on the weak and defenceless, only willing to attack people when you're in a group, not at risk yourself. Just another bully."

"Your family wouldn't have wanted you to give up, Jozef. They would have wanted you to live. You need to leave Germany."

"How do you propose I do that? I've no money and no papers. I'd be picked up within hours."

"Wait here. I'll go fetch my skis for you. You can go up into the mountains and into Austria. It's not that far from there to Switzerland. Just stay up high until you get there. That way they won't catch you." Jozef said nothing. "Stay in Germany and you'll probably die."

Still Jozef made no comment.

"Well?" Jozef gave an almost imperceptible nod. "I'll be back within an hour."

Torsten returned with his winter coat, hat, and gloves as well as the skis and a backpack for Jozef. "You'll find food in there and a shovel, so that you can dig yourself a snow hole at night to keep warm like Herr Brandt showed us."

Jozef remained silent. He put on the coat, took the other items and walked past Torsten to the door. Torsten opened his mouth to say good luck, but Jozef had already merged with the night.

Walking back home, Torsten halted frequently and gazed up at the slopes to see if he could spot Jozef silhouetted against the snow on the mountains, but he couldn't. Doubtless he was sticking to the forested areas. A wise precaution.

Anxiety gnawed at Torsten's gut. He hoped that if Jozef was caught, he wouldn't tell them that he, Torsten, had helped him escape. And even if Jozef didn't talk, what if they traced the skis back to him? Oh well, it was too late to worry about that. What was done was done.

Soon eighteen, Torsten was conscripted into the army. When in September 1939 Hitler invaded Poland, Britain and France declared war. In 1940, German troops swept through Europe conquering Denmark, Norway, Holland, Belgium and France with ease. The worries of those in Germany about the wisdom of another war were quickly forgotten.

Torsten, who had been stationed in France, was given leave for Christmas. Franz too came home. Their mother gave them the latest family news as they sat by the fire on Tortsen's first night home.

"Ingrid got married a couple of weeks ago. Kurt, her husband, is an officer in the Gestapo. Your father and I went to the wedding in Berlin. Heinrich Himmler, head of the Gestapo, attended. It was a very grand affair. I wish you could both have been there to see it."

"Are they coming here for Christmas?"

Torsten fervently hoped so, he hadn't seen his sister for five years now.

"No, unfortunately Kurt's duties prevent that."

Torsten wondered when he would finally get to

see Ingrid again. He'd soon be back at the front, such as that was. There was no further to go unless Hitler gave orders to cross the English Channel.

"I think he may not bother," said Gruber as the family sat eating their Christmas dinner. "After all, the English pose no threat. Despite all their lies and deceit, they can't persuade the Americans to join the war, and without them they don't have the power to attack us. It's Russia that's the real danger."

"But we have a pact with them. We divided up Poland between us," said Torsten.

"That is so, but we depend on them for our oil and other raw materials, and for their grain to keep us fed. If they cut all that off, the Reich would be in jeopardy. The Soviets can't be trusted. They're communists, bent on world domination. The Führer would be doing western civilisation a great service if he attacked them. Those Slavs are subhuman like the Jews. And with Russia defeated, it would be too late for America to enter the war and England would be forced to make peace."

"I totally agree with father," said Franz. "And our forces are far superior. Their army is just a motley collection of peasants with horses."

"Can we forget about the war for just one day?" sighed Frau Gruber. "Let's enjoy all being together. We don't know when the next time will be."

"I have a surprise for you, Mutti." Torsten reached inside his jacket pocket and handed her his gift.

His mother unwrapped it. "Fine stockings pur-

chased on the boulevards of Paris."
"Ah, thank you. Come give your mother a kiss."
"I have something too," said his brother.
"Oh, Franz. Perfume. I'm being spoiled."
"And a vintage cognac for you, Papa."
"Thank you Franz. We must also give thanks to the Führer. Now we control all these countries, he is having their produce and goods shipped to Germany. So you see, every German citizen benefits from this war. A war we will soon win."
"Oh Wolfgang, let it rest, can't you. No more politics until tomorrow at least. Please."
It was the last Christmas Torsten would ever spend with his family, the last that he would ever spend in the cosy confines of his beloved valley beneath those snowy peaks.

CHAPTER 14

A wide smile illuminated Torsten's face. It wasn't only thanks to the warm summer sunshine making him feel happy. It was the unexpected welcome. A young woman had just jumped up onto the treads of his stationary tank and kissed him as he leaned forward from the open hatch to accept her offering of wild flowers.

For several kilometres now as the long line of tanks and vehicles had driven along the rutted road, locals had greeted them, waving and cheering. It wasn't at all what Torsten had anticipated when the largest invasion force in history of over three and a half million men had attacked Russia a few weeks earlier. Maybe Hitler and his stepfather had been right that this would end the war.

"Don't expect this to last," commented Klaus, another of the tank crew. "These country folk are glad to be rid of the Soviets because they wouldn't let them grow food for themselves. The Commies pushed everyone onto collective farms to meet state quotas. Let people starve even. These people think we've come to liberate them. They won't be so happy when they find out that we'll be taking their food to feed ourselves without any concern about whether they'll have enough left to survive."

A shot rang out. One of the German infantry behind them fell to the ground, fatally wounded. In seconds, the bucolic scene had turned to carnage as German soldiers began spraying those watching them pass with bullets. Others aimed their flame throwers at the village houses, not stopping until every dwelling was on fire.

Black smoke billowed upwards, blocking out the sun. There were no more cheers, no more laughing. Desolate cries of grief had pushed them aside. All had turned from heaven to hell in the space of only a minute or two.

When later that day hundreds of Russian soldiers appeared, hands in the air in surrender, Torsten and his colleagues were commanded to open fire on them. They fell like dominoes, too shocked to try and run. It would take too long to pull the bodies off the road so the tanks flattened them as they led the way forward.

"We don't want prisoners. Our whole effort must be on moving forward, nothing else," their commander had said.

And so it was all along the hundreds of kilometres that constituted the Russian front, a line that stretched from the Baltic in the North to the Black Sea in the South. On and on the Germans went, scoring victory after victory.

They were well equipped with the latest military hardware. Often the Russians sent into battle against them were unarmed, told to pick guns from dead Germans, told that if they retreated they would be shot as deserters. Some even lacked shoes, their feet wrapped in pieces of cloth. The Nazis were unstoppable, a plague of death and suffering. Their adversary was no match for them. Yet still there was more land to cross to get to Moscow. Russia was a place like no other. Vast, endless. It sucked them in, further and further until they lost all sense of how far they'd come.

At night as he lay under the stars, Torsten wondered how far away home now was. One thousand, two thousand kilometres, maybe more.

The stars still looked the same, but when dawn washed them from the sky, there would be no mountain peaks or tranquil meadows calling him to walk amongst them, no immaculately maintained chalets to retreat to at the end of they day. Instead, he would wake to vast plains, much of which would be black like coal from Hitler's scorched earth policy. Birdsong would be replaced by shells exploding, screams, and cries for help. How he longed to be back home in Bavaria, away from this dystopian world.

Initially shocked by the brutality that they were expected to display, over time he became immune to it. He didn't give it much of a thought any longer. He couldn't. How could he cope otherwise. Like the rest he was focussed on one thing and one thing only, reaching Moscow.

"Not long now lads. In just a few weeks we'll be there in the capital. At the gates of the Kremlin, smashing it to smithereens and the war will be over. Then you'll be able to go home to a heroes' welcome and get on with your lives," their commander assured them.

Torsten believed every word, they all did. It gave them the will to go on, to know that there would only be a few more weeks of this. Hitler had taken Western Europe with ease, so why not Russia. After all, the armies of Britain and France had been much better equipped.

But seasons change. Summer living had been easy. Then the rains of autumn came. There were no autobahns here. The tracks turned to mud and became impassable quagmires. Sinking up to their knees trying to free vehicles, the invaders' progress halted. Days of wet feet and soggy clothes turned into weeks.

"Let's hope it freezes soon," said Klaus.

And it did. On a hardened surface, moving forward became easier. They were so close to Moscow now, they could see it there on the horizon. Just one final push. That was all that was needed. Napoleon had failed in his invasion of Russia, but they wouldn't. They were the master race.

But here winter wasn't like Bavaria, bringing rosy cheeks and good cheer. Here winter was vicious, an enemy stronger than any that they had previously encountered.

Fuel froze, engines cracked. Their reliance on

modern machines had gone from being an advantage to a weakness.

Supply lines faltered. Torsten and his compatriots shivered. Winter clothes didn't arrive. They resorted to stuffing newspaper and straw inside their boots and uniforms in an effort to keep warm. At thirty and forty below it didn't help much. As Klaus spat one day, his spittle froze before it touched the ground.

Like a sitting duck, Torsten's stranded tank was picked off. The crew were able to get out and flee. Like thousands of others they retreated.

Russian commandos dressed in quilted suits and on skis would suddenly appear out of the thick forest, harassing them remorselessly. Things were slowly but surely turning in Stalin's favour.

At last, Russia had started to get its act together. In factories relocated east of Moscow to be out of reach of German bombers, tanks and aircraft were rolling off the production line at a far faster rate than Germany could hope to emulate.

Klaus and Torsten became separated from their unit. In the heavily falling snow there was no sun to give any clue of direction. They were utterly lost. That night, they dug a snow hole. Lighting a fire was too dangerous. The enemy could be anywhere, attack from any direction, and then retreat into the forest until the next night.

"How I wish I was back in Berlin. Strolling along Unter den Linden arm in arm with a lovely girl. Where did it all go wrong? Hitler has led us through the gates of hell."

"You shouldn't talk like that, Klaus. The SS have ears everywhere."

"Let them kill me if they want. But I doubt they will. They need us to fight. Fight their fucking stupid war. And what choice do we have? You saw what they ordered us to do to the Russians as we advanced. If we surrender, they'll rip us apart like rabid dogs. Our commanders know that, know that we must fight to the death. Fighting is the only possible way we might survive."

Next morning as they emerged from their snow hole cautiously like bear cubs hoping to find their mother to protect them, they saw two other German soldiers up ahead sitting in the snow with their backs to them not far away.

"Hey, we've lost our way. Do you know where we are?" called Torsten.

The soldiers didn't react. Once Torsten and Klaus reached them, they saw why. The two men had frozen to death overnight. They had become grim ice sculptures, icicles hanging from their beards. No one shaved any longer. There was precious little opportunity to do so, and facial hair provided some protection from the elements.

Like human vultures, the two companions scavenged what they could from the dead men. Their gloves and their coats. But they were as stiff as board and the morning sun didn't melt them. Before long, they had dumped them. It was just extra weight to carry.

Hunger gnawed at them and thirst tormented them. However, eating snow only gave them stomach ache.

All that day they stumbled through deep snow. It was a long time since they had felt any sensation in their extremities. Their fingers and feet were numb, their faces bright red from being burned in the icy winds. Even in the forests, which they clung to whenever they could, that wind would find them, blowing up snow all around them as though it were snowing even when it wasn't. Each time they inhaled, it was as if the icy tentacles of death's foot soldiers were reaching deep into their lungs, remorselessly seeking the route to their hearts so they could tighten around them and stop them beating.

Late that afternoon they heard howls. The wind had dropped and the clouds had cleared. If it weren't so life threateningly cold, it would have been beautiful. The sun, now a big orange ball sinking towards the horizon, was peeping through the tree trunks, tantalisingly promising a warmth that it didn't deliver.

Torsten and Klaus were unnerved by the howls. Those primeval noises were repeated more often than earlier and sounded closer than before.

"Let's dig a hole and hide," said Klaus.

"You can't hide. They can probably smell us for miles."

"Well, we need to dig a snow hole anyway and get some shelter."

They found a drift that looked promising. With their hands, they began to claw away. The top of the snow was encrusted with ice. It was exhausting work.

The cold and lack of food took its toll. Their actions were slow and often clumsy. It was well after nightfall by the time they had constructed a rudimentary snow cave. From the inside, they piled up snow in the entrance leaving only a small gap so that they wouldn't suffocate from lack of oxygen. They had equipped themselves with branches, the only weapon which they had apart from their short knives to ward off attack. Their pistols had already jammed with the freezing temperatures.

They barely slept. Even huddled together in a small space it remained bitterly cold, just less so than on the outside. All night long intermittent, mournful cries woke them whenever they dozed, though so far as they knew the wolves never approached.

Come morning, Klaus took off one of his boots and his sock to rub his foot.

"Oh my God. Look at my toes." His toes were swollen and discoloured, a ghostly mixture of white and blue with a little black. "I've got frostbite." He pulled off the other boot. "On both feet. Shit."

"It'll be OK. We'll find our army today, I'm sure."

"You should check yours."

"There's no point. It won't change anything. Come on, we should get going."

Torsten was scared to look. He didn't want to

know. There was nothing he could do about it if he too had frostbite. He would continue hoping that he hadn't. He dreaded the prospect of losing his feet and becoming a cripple like his father.

Not long after leaving they came across the bodies of three Russian soldiers, or what remained of them, which was only carcass and torn garments. The snow around them was stained crimson. The wolves must have found them. Doubtless already dead, it was an easier meal than seeking something living. The wolves too had to conserve their energy and not waste it on a failed chase. A Russian winter was a desperate time for man and animal alike.

Klaus and Torsten were luckier than many. They found the German army the following day and lived. Klaus had to have his toes amputated, but the rest of his feet were saved and he got sent back to Germany. Torsten sometimes wished that he had suffered the same fate. His feet were undamaged so he was pronounced fit and could spend more years fighting.

Torsten's life was passing him by in a barely remembered haze of killing and others trying to kill him. At times, he wished the Russians would get him. There seemed no point to his existence any longer. What was it all for? Each new dawn brought bowel loosening fear and only the promise of new horrors. There was no hope of a better tomorrow.

By now he should have had a wife, or a girlfriend

at least, and maybe his own home. If it hadn't been for this damn war and the hijacking of his country by fanatics, he could have been experiencing a pleasant and fulfilling life as a shoe maker or ski instructor, perhaps even both. A peaceful life, surrounded by mountains and fields and cocooned in laughter and kisses.

On Christmas Eve, the soldiers Torsten was with came upon an old wooden church which had somehow survived when nearly everything around it had been razed to the ground. The villagers had built a crude new altar when the communists had ripped out the interior some years ago.

That evening they had brought in icons which they had hidden to avoid them being seized. Mainly elderly, they were kneeling before the altar praying in the light of a solitary candle. They looked terrified when they turned their heads upon hearing footsteps and saw those uniforms, to them an omen of death. Close to starving, their faces were gaunt, their eyes sunken into their sockets like tortured souls in a Goya painting.

For once the soldiers smiled at them, but the congregation remained unnerved. Clutching their relics to their chests, they got up and moved down one wall and out into the night, disappearing into the forest where they were trying to survive.

The soldiers remained, wanting to absorb some serenity. A precious few moments of peace. A few minutes when they could forget the violence and

hatred that consumed every day of their lives.
One began singing Heilige Nacht, Silent Night. The others joined in. Tears coursed freely down their faces. Whether they were tears of pity or guilt, or tears of self pity, only each man knew his answer to that question.
By the end of 1943, Germany was in full retreat. Hitler's gamble had failed. The Russian army was only two hundred kilometres from the Polish border, its goal Berlin. As for Torsten, he was already behind the lines.

CHAPTER 15

The Russians had raided at night. Shot Torsten in the right leg. It had hurt like hell but maybe he should be happy about it. He was away from the front. They said he would walk with a limp for quite a while, but he still had both his legs. That made him more fortunate than countless thousands of others.

Torsten was in a military hospital near Lublin in Poland. Lying on a proper bed after so much time felt luxurious. Not always being permanently tired from sleeping fitfully in case of attack was sheer bliss. Not to mention having sheets and blankets.

And he was finally clean again. No longer did he have to exist in the same clothes for weeks on end. In the Russian winters, personal hygiene had been a challenge. Any water was encased under thick ice and that which could be extracted was much too cold to have a proper wash in. Rare had been the occasions when there had been the opportunity of warming it.

"I have a visitor here to see you," said a nurse, stepping aside to reveal someone Torsten hadn't expected to see.

"Franz? What are you doing here?" Torsten sat up in bed.

"I'm in charge of a work camp nearby. Mutti wrote to tell me you were here when she got your letter and asked me to visit you. How are you?"

His tone was more one of indifference than concern.

"It's still a little painful. They say I'll be up and walking in a few days."

"And then what?"

"I haven't been told. Hopefully not back to the front."

"You could come and work as a guard at the camp. There's plenty of chaps who've been stationed there after being wounded in battle. I could arrange it for you. It's not demanding work, merely keeping an eye on the prisoners and making sure that they don't escape."

"Russians?"

"Yes, and a few others."

"OK then, I will. Have you been home at all?"

"Yes, I got to go last Christmas."

"And Ingrid. Was she there?"

"No, but still very happy in Berlin by all accounts."

"Has Partenkirchen been effected by the war?"

"Not really, it's still as beautiful as ever."

"Ah, how I long to get back there."

"You will, but first we must win this war."

Remembering how fervent a supporter of Hitler his brother had been, Torsten stifled a snort of disbelief. Tired of pleasantries, his brother made to go.

"I'll see you soon. Heil Hitler."

Franz still said those words with conviction and enthusiasm, and thrust his arm out with certainty and pride. It seemed clear that his views hadn't changed one iota.

The term work camp proved to be a euphemism of the first order. The place was horrific beyond imagination.

Whilst Torsten was assigned watch tower duty, he soon understood what was going on here. It was evident from the skeletal figures in striped pyjamas whose eyes looked as if they were already dead. Devoid of hope or emotion as they stood behind the barbed wire fence the day he arrived. It was also evident from the unpleasant stench and from the smoke rising from the oven chimneys. This was no work camp. It was a death camp.

Once more Torsten felt the bile rise in his throat. It was Kristallnacht all over again but on a scale many thousands of times worse. He wanted to leave, but he knew he couldn't ask his brother. He'd be called out as unreliable, a danger to the Reich. And what good would it do? It wouldn't save one life.

Torsten had made a pact with the devil many years ago as had all the millions who had joined the Hitler Youth. True, they had been indoctrinated. Membership for many had been compulsory, not wished for. But how much of an excuse was that now, or had it been in Russia, or even on Kristallnacht? Torsten had played his part. The collective whole was the sum of the acts of each individual, each of them absolving themselves from any culpability by thinking what they did or didn't do would make no difference.

Torsten rarely got to see his brother, save from a distance. Maybe he was too busy, or worried about what others would think, concerned about accusations of nepotism. Not that Torsten cared. His brother was hateful. And thinking that deflected his own part in the killing machine. Although he may not have led people to their death, he guarded the camp's perimeters to stop victims escaping.

Franz did send for Torsten once. He was sitting in his office, his eyes red as though he'd been crying.

"Mutti's dead."

"How? When?"

"What does that matter, she's gone."

"But-"

"Leave."

Torsten hesitated.

"I'm your commanding officer here. That was an order. Get out."

Torsten had to hold his grief until that night after lights out in the barracks. He cried in silence. The two women in his life were gone. His mother dead, his sister unreachable. They had nurtured him and cared for him. They had been the only thing in his life that wasn't harsh and unyielding. They had been a softness, a gentleness that he hardly remembered any longer in this hard, unforgiving existence that ground you down and kept its boot firmly on your neck.

It was a heavy blow. He no longer had a family. Torsten was alone in the world. He didn't consider his brother as family any longer.

One evening some weeks later as Torsten wandered back to the barracks, he saw him pass. It had to be him. It could only be him.

"Hey, you. Stop."

The prisoner did as commanded.

His face was thin and drawn. The man looked much older than the twenty-six or twenty-seven years he must now be. But there was no mistake. It was him.

Torsten looked around furtively. No other guards were nearby.

"Jozef. They caught you?"

Jozef leaned forward, peering in the fading light.

"It's me, Torsten."

"Oh. As you see, they did. They sent me here. After years of slave labour in Germany. Now I help sort through the valuables of new arrivals when they get here. Until no more arrive or I collapse from hunger. Then I'll be sent to the gas chambers too."

He spoke in a monotone, matter of fact way as though they were just discussing today's weather.

"Will that be all?"

"Er...yes."

Jozef shuffled away. Torsten shook his head and

went off to the warmth of the barracks where prisoners would serve him a hot meal, something which they could only smell, never eat.

One of the women guards supervised them in the kitchen. Beady eyed like an eagle, ready to pounce if any took food. Only yesterday, she had shot dead a prisoner who had thought her back was turned when he took but a mouthful.

Torsten had been more shocked to see that many of the guards here were women and to discover that they were as ruthless as the men than realising it was an extermination camp.

The talk at dinner was of the Russian advance.

"I've heard say they could be here in a few days," said one, slurping on his soup and letting out a long burp.

"I overheard Drexler telling another officer that he'd received orders for us to move out in the next day or two. March the prisoners west to Auschwitz. Said most would probably die on the way so that will save some work when we get there," added another. "Those too weak to walk will be eliminated before we leave."

That night Torsten lay awake in his bed thinking. If they went west hopefully the American or British army would reach them before the Russians. He'd have a better chance of surviving that way.

He thought back to his childhood too, of all that had happened. Of the day that he had been saved from the bullies.

The following evening, he went for a walk after

dark. He would be on duty later tonight. Him and one other.

He had noticed which of the long low wooden huts Jozef had entered. Torsten went in. Tens were crammed onto rudimentary bunks. There were no mattresses, no covers, no pillows. The air was stale and smelt of body odour. Numerous pairs of eyes followed him as he walked along the narrow space between the two lines of bunk beds.

“Messing. Jozef Messing?” he asked.

A man silently pointed.

“Come with me.”

Jozef climbed down from a top bunk. The others gave him that look, one which said that they didn’t expect to see him again.

CHAPTER 16

Torsten took him down the side of the building, out of sight of the watchtower and its rotating searchlight.

"They're going to march you to Auschwitz before the Russians get here. Those that don't die on the way, they'll kill when they get there. I'm on duty tonight. I'm going to cut a hole in the fence, over there." He pointed to the spot. "When the guard with me up in the tower takes a break, I'll switch the searchlight off temporarily. You'll have a chance to get out. Go East, the Russians can't be far away. Take as many with you as you can."

"You know that they'll kill you for this."

"They won't know I did it."

Jozef walked away, but then turned.

"Thank you."

"There's nothing to thank me for. You were a true friend. I let you down. Now get back in before anyone sees us." When Jozef had gone, Torsten double checked that no one else was in the vicinity and once the beam of light had passed, he raced over to the fence and cut the lowest line of barbed wire in two places.

That evening he stood up in the watch tower, waiting. It was well gone midnight until the guard he was on duty with excused himself for a few minutes. Once he had left and entered the barracks, Torsten shut off the beam.

He hoped Jozef was ready to go. He didn't intend to leave if off for long. If the other guard came out before he put it back on, saying that the spotlight had malfunctioned would sound extremely suspicious once any escape was discovered.

Torsten could only wait a few minutes. They would just have to be quick. He ground his clammy palms together, counting the seconds.

Right. Time to turn it back on. The beam was just passing the opening in the fence as he did so. Torsten thought that he could see people still waiting to get under, but the beam had moved on. When it reached that point again, there was nothing to see.

He smiled. Surely he'd done it. Freed Jozef and hopefully many more.

At the early morning briefing, he stood to attention with the other guards as his brother gave orders. They were moving out that very morning.

At roll call no one from Jozef's hut emerged. Franz was enraged.

"Get them out. Now!"

Two female guards hurried over. Torsten noticed Franz had removed his pistol from its holster, doubtless determined to shoot some of them who remained for being late.

Moments later, the two women returned holding

a man under his arms and dragging him along. He was clearly too sick to walk unaided.

"They've all gone apart from this one," said one of the women.

"What do you mean they've gone?" Franz's face had become puce with fury.

"Their beds are empty."

"What happened?" Franz demanded of the man.

He said nothing.

"You will answer me!"

He struck his head with his pistol. The man's forehead began bleeding from the gash inflicted and his head flopped forward. Franz shot him and the women let him fall to the ground as though they had accidentally picked up a piece of dog shit.

"Excuse me, sir."

A nervous voice spoke up from the rank of prisoners.

"Who spoke?"

A man stepped forward.

"Well?"

"I'm in the hut next door. I overheard a guard talking to a prisoner last night, saying he was going to cut a hole in the fence. That he would be on guard in the watch tower and switch off the searchlight."

"Did you see him?"

"No, sir. I could only hear him."

"Well, you're no help, are you."

Franz shot him in the chest at close range.

"Who was on duty last night?"

"Me," said Torsten.

"And me," said the man who had been with him.

"Come with me. The rest of you carry on and get ready to leave."

Franz led them into his office and slammed the door shut.

"It was me who cut the barbed wire," said Torsten.

Franz stood next to the other guard and shot him in the head. His legs folded under him and he fell onto the floor, dead.

"What the fuck did you do that for?"

It wasn't even seven o'clock and already this morning his brother had murdered three innocent men in cold blood.

"So he won't talk. Why did you do it, Torsten? Bring disgrace upon the family name. Why?"

Franz spat out the words with rage. Coming right up to his brother, he positioned his pistol against the side of Torsten's head. Torsten could feel the pressure of the metal on his temple. He had survived years on the Russian front only for his own brother to kill him.

"Why? Answer me, damn you!"

Franz pulled back the trigger a little. Torsten, who had been feeling nauseous with fear, suddenly didn't any longer. He was going to die. What more was there to be frightened of?

"Because I'm sick of all the killing. Look at you, Franz. Look at what you've become. A murderer, a mass murderer."

"Nonsense. These Jews, these Russians, the gypsies, they're not human. You've betrayed the Fatherland. I should shoot you on the spot. But no, that would be too easy for you." Franz withdrew his gun. "You can stay here. Let the Russians have you. They can torture you and then kill you, or maybe they'll work you to death in a labour camp. Either way you'll die and I don't care. You're not my brother anymore. You're scum, just like the Jews."

Then to Torsten's surprise, Franz fired his gun.

CHAPTER 17

Though the bullet went into the floor, Torsten couldn't help but jump.

"What a miserable traitor you are." Franz shook his head with contempt and left.

Torsten slumped into the chair by the desk, drained and exhausted from the ordeal. From outside, came frantic shouting and commands. They were in a hurry to leave. The Russians must be close.

Torsten looked through the window. The guards were herding prisoners through the gates, screaming at them to move faster. Franz was getting into his car. His driver sounded his horn repeatedly, forcing his way past guards and prisoners.

Soon they had all gone and Torsten came out. A few prisoners who had hidden in the confusion of the rushed departure, and those too weak to go who hadn't already been shot, sat on the ground or walked aimlessly about.

Some looked at the open gates, though none went towards them. Had the brutality here robbed them of all independent will or were they waiting for rescue, putting their faith in the Russians? Torsten didn't know.

Many looked bewildered to see him still alive, others ignored him. He approached some of them.

"Come."

None moved. It appeared they didn't trust him. How could he blame them? He walked across to the barracks and went inside. He came out with a plate on which was bread, cheese and cold meat.

"Come with me. Come eat."

Several followed him, others waited still not convinced.

Those who entered, he asked to sit down. Torsten brought out the food which he had found in the kitchen, putting it on the table and watched them devour it.

When it was gone, he got some more and asked them to give it to those who had remained outside. Torsten stayed where he was. Sitting on a bench, he put his elbows on the table and his head into his hands.

What should he do? Wait for the Russians? Wait for them to shoot him, or attempt to reach the front line in the west and surrender and perhaps be shot by his own army as he tried to get there? Going west surely offered the best chance of survival. After all these years of war and managing to cheat death on many occasions if he could just stay alive a few more months, it could all be over. What would a year or two in a prisoner of war camp matter? Once the war ended, they surely wouldn't keep him interned for long.

Torsten was well into his twenties now. His youth had been spent preparing for war or fighting it. He wanted it all to be over. After a spell as a POW, he would be able to go home and build a life, a normal life.

Torsten made his way over to the building where new prisoners due for immediate annihilation were taken. Inside, clothes and shoes were piled high. He stripped off, discarding his uniform. Torsten expected thousands of civilians would now be moving west, seeking to stay one step ahead of the Russians. He would dress as a refugee and become incognito in the crowds.

Torsten took some clothing and put it on. The trousers were a little short, the shirt tight, the jacket loose. It didn't matter, they would suffice. However, it took him several attempts to find a pair of shoes that fitted well enough to walk in for any length of time.

He picked up a small suitcase from a stack of bags and cases. It wasn't properly closed and a small, worn teddy bear fell out of it as it opened.

He would return to the barracks and put some provisions inside. Food on the journey Torsten had to make was likely to be in short supply, plus he could also use it to barter with or bribe if the need arose. To cross Poland and then Germany was several hundred kilometres. He hoped the Americans and British were advancing fast in his direction.

Stepping outside, his heart missed a beat. He stopped in his tracks. A vehicle was coming through the gates with soldiers on foot following. Quickly, he retreated back inside.

Going through the door at the back into another room, he came face to face with the results of the barbarity practised here. Naked bodies were heaped on one another, their faces contorted in agony. Bodies which hadn't yet been burned. In death as in life they hadn't been afforded any dignity. Guilty of nothing, they had been treated worse than animals.

For a moment, he couldn't move. Torsten had seen so many horrors, so many dead, but not an enormous heap of corpses like this, piled high as if just so much garbage. The sound of boots echoing off the floor in the next room galvanised him into action. The door opened.

In a panic, Torsten squeezed himself between the bodies and the wall, trying to bury himself amongst the dead until the Russians had gone. The victims were cold and so pitifully thin that he could feel their bones pressing against him.

The soldiers were thorough. They found him cowering there and dragged him out. Two took him outside to where a group of prisoners were standing.

The Soviet commander said something. One of the inmates translated into German for the others.

"He says do we know this man. Is he a German soldier?"

"Yes, he was one of the guards."

The first man translated. The commander raised his gun to shoot Torsten. He closed his eyes. This was it, there was nothing he could do.

"No, stop!" another prisoner shouted. "He is a good man. He cut a hole in the fence for us last night and many escaped. He doesn't deserve to die."

After hearing the translation, the commander let his arm fall. He said something to the soldiers with him who marched Torsten brusquely out of the camp.

CHAPTER 18

The light was intense. Torsten had his eyes almost closed in an effort to reduce the brightness. Something shimmered on the horizon. He quickened his pace.

It was a lake. Cool waters that beckoned, promising relief from the unrelenting heat. Others saw it too and walked faster. But as they got closer, it disappeared. It had been but a mirage that had merely toyed with them.

Torsten felt light headed in the scorching summer sun. Putting one foot in front of the other was becoming increasingly difficult. He wondered if it might have been better if they had shot him, rather than lead him towards a slow, lingering death. Mainly though his mind was consumed with the thought of water. How he craved a sip, to feel it wet his parched mouth and slip like nectar down his throat.

For three days now they had walked, he and what seemed an unending line of German prisoners of war. Those who fell over were shot and left where they fell, or sometimes just left. They would die anyway and why waste a bullet.

They hadn't been fed or given any water. Only when they came upon a lake or a river could they drink, falling to their knees and gulping down as much as they could like wild animals, not knowing when the next opportunity to quench their thirst might arrive.

He could hear grumblings about their inhumane treatment, but he knew that they had treated the Russians worse. Torsten was surprised that they hadn't all been shot. After all that is what the Germans had almost invariably done when Russians had surrendered.

How much further they had to go, he didn't know. The soldiers told them nothing. A couple of times a day they were allowed to rest while the soldiers ate. At night, they got to lay on the baked, uneven earth that made them ache in whatever position they lay. If it had been winter, they would all have been dead by now.

As they walked, they could observe once more the destruction which they had inflicted all over this land. Charred remains of where villages had stood, piles of rubble where towns had once been.

Hitler had underestimated the Russian people. He had regarded them as inferior, barely human. An easy foe to conquer. They had proved him wrong, proved to be extremely tough and endlessly resilient. Now they would be his downfall and that of Germany.

Mother Russia consumed the prisoners in her unending steppes. Torsten knew that he would never be able to leave her embrace unless permitted to. Their guards didn't bother to watch them at night. Where could they run to? They were subsumed in her huge expanse. If a man ran, the locals would surely tear him limb from limb for the death and misery the Nazis had inflicted upon every family in this land.

They reached a small station standing all alone on the flat landscape. The community it served had been bombed to oblivion. Some, including Torsten, were pulled aside while the rest were left to march on.

While they sat listlessly on the platform in the unforgiving sun as flies pestered them, their guards played cards in the shade of the half of the waiting room that wasn't a pile of broken concrete. Torsten's tongue was as dry as desert sand. When he swallowed, his throat was gritty from the absolute absence of any moisture in his mouth. Each minute seemed like an hour.

A noise began. At first it was vague, uncertain. As it grew in strength, it resonated from the railway tracks becoming rhythmical and loud.

Belching acrid smoke into the air, which stung their eyes as it engulfed them, a train arrived. They were herded into windowless wagons. Packed in tightly, there was no room to sit. Just as the Germans had treated the Jews and others, now it was their turn. Soon the air inside smelled foul from their sweat and bodily functions.

At one stop hours later, the sliding doors of the

wagons were opened and the men were hosed down. Each strained forward to catch some of the water in his mouth. Stale bread was thrown at them. They all pushed and fought to get a piece. Then the light was shut out once again and the train rumbled slowly off.

Reaching their destination the following day, they stepped out disoriented. It appeared that they had arrived on the outskirts of a city. Marched to an open air compound fenced by barbed wire, they were allowed to sit. Torsten assumed that they must have reached a death camp, to be gassed or otherwise killed like the Nazis had so ruthlessly and systematically. Yet come evening as the guards circulated amongst them, they threw a raw potato at each man. Torsten didn't even try to get the dirt off before he bit into his, so great was his hunger.

"What do you think's going to happen to us?" asked a man near him.

"We're on the outskirts of Moscow from what I can tell," said another. "Maybe we're here to help them rebuild. Free labour for them."

Early next morning before it was properly light, they were woken by kicks from the guards and made to form lines of twenty wide before being marched out of the compound and into the city. Citizens lined the streets. Most jeered, some threw stones and small rocks. One hit Torsten on the back of the head. There was blood on his hand after he'd felt the spot where he'd been hit. On their flanks, Russian soldiers marched along side them, toting their guns.

Torsten recognised the colourful domes of St Basil's Cathedral when they were marched into the huge space of Red Square itself. It was as if the domes were made from sticks of candy, each a set of stripes in different colours. Their shape seemed more Arabian than European, like an Ottoman Sultan's turban.

He wondered if it was the reddish brown of the buildings and walls enclosing the square which had given it its name, or whether it was named after the "Reds", the communists. In fact it was neither, it derived from the old Russian word "krasny" which meant beautiful and has come to mean red in modern Russian.

In this huge space Torsten felt like an ant, an ant who could be squashed at will should the central figure on the podium which they had to march past desire it. Like a Roman emperor in the Colosseum, Stalin stood there with members of his government watching with undisguised satisfaction. He sported a moustache which was wider and thicker than Hitler's. An avuncular look suggested a warm and friendly personality. Something that Hitler's mad-eyed appearance never conveyed, though in reality Uncle Joe wore only a tiger's smile.

That July day in 1944, over fifty thousand German prisoners were paraded through Moscow. Dirty and dishevelled, they were a symbol of the vanquished. A powerful message to the Russian people that their huge sacrifice, which would total over twenty-five million dead by the war's end, had been worthwhile. A tangible confirmation that the Soviet Union and communism had triumphed over fascism.

Back at the compound the prisoners all wondered what their fate would now be. Had they served their purpose? Stalin killed his own people in vast numbers without a second thought. The life of these Germans could be of absolutely no interest to him.

The following morning, they were broken into smaller groups and taken to camps around the city. Here they were first required to build huts that would become their homes. During the weeks and months that followed, they were taken out to various locations to clear rubble and dig foundations for new buildings that would take the place of those which they had destroyed during their failed invasion.

In the evenings before they were permitted to eat, commissars gave lectures on the evils of capitalism and the shining future of socialism. As the months passed they learned of Hitler's suicide, Germany's unconditional surrender, and the satellite communist states being established the length of Eastern Europe, including one half of what had been Germany. Only two countries had emerged stronger from the most violent conflict in history, the United States and Russia.

Russian lessons were offered and Torsten seized the chance to learn. It appeared likely that they would be here for a very long time, if not forever.

CHAPTER 19

"You are an exemplary worker, Comrade Drexler, and the Party has noted your efforts."

Sergei Orlov, the head of the plant gave a rare smile as he and Torsten stood in Orlov's office overlooking the factory floor. Though it was already some years since the war had ended, Orlov still dressed in military uniform, a row of medals pinned on his chest. Lines of worry and hardship from the war years like rivers on a map were etched upon his face, but now he enjoyed the fruits of victory. A war hero, he was a rising star in the Communist Party

When Torsten had begun working there, Orlov hadn't even acknowledged him. However, his strong work ethic had made him stand out from the crowd, especially the Russian workers who did the minimum that they possibly could. They had little incentive to do otherwise. Everyone got paid the same, save for POWs who got nothing.

"How would you feel about being promoted to be one of my deputies?"

"I've never thought about it. Never expected it."

"There would be privileges. You would be allowed

to live in an apartment in recognition of your efforts."

It had been over five years since Torsten had arrived in Moscow, five bleak years. After three years of working outside as a labourer, he had been transferred to work in this armaments factory. It was dull and repetitive but at least he now worked indoors, protected to a degree from the extremes of the Russian climate.

The news thrilled him. At last he would be out of the camp, living a life that was normal, or as normal as it was likely to ever get.

"You would be paid. There is just one formality. You would need to become a Soviet citizen."

Become Russian, that was something Torsten had also never thought about. But what was there to consider? There seemed little chance that he'd ever be going home. No one at his camp had yet been released. They worked them until they died, and many had from the tough conditions. As a citizen he would have benefits, get holiday leave, receive a pension when he reached retirement age. Life would have some hope, the prospect of a better tomorrow.

"It would be an honour, Comrade Orlov."

The apartment was in a block not far from the factory. Like most Moscow apartments, other than those reserved for the Communist Party elite, it was dowdy and poorly maintained.

He was introduced by Orlov to the Residents' Committee as a good worker and loyal supporter of the Party. Torsten found his fate ironic. He had given up his forced allegiance to one dictator for another. Still, if he kept his head down he would have a better future than he had anticipated.

He shared the bedroom with another worker. There was a small living room come kitchen. The bathroom was down the hall, used also by four other apartments. However, compared to the camp it was the height of comfort. He had a bed with a mattress, not straw. In winter, there was heating and warm water. There was a sofa to sit on, a table to eat off and a radio to listen to the state controlled station.

And there was money to buy food, albeit he would have to stand patiently in long lines with everyone else for whatever might happen to be available on any particular day. Even when he reached the front of the line, there was more waiting involved. Issued with a ticket, he then had to wait in line at the cashier's to pay and get a receipt, before queueing a third time to present the receipt in exchange for the food he had purchased.

Yet above all, there was some freedom. Freedom on his day off on a Sunday to wander the capital's streets.

Torsten explored the city that now was to be his long term home. Travel on the underground was cheap and a destination in itself. Away from Red Square and the Kremlin, most of the city was ugly, a landscape of grey concrete and smoke stacks, but here beneath the surface it was a different world.

Stalin had ordered that the Moscow Metro be constructed as 'palaces for the people'. For a population starved of luxury, they must truly have seemed such with their wide corridors and numerous arches, the generous use of marble and large chandeliers. There were enormous bronze statues, stained glass windows and huge Byzantine-style mosaics. However, instead of religious figures they depicted the Soviet gods, Stalin and Lenin, and scenes from Russia's past as well as murals of farmers, soldiers and students, all in strident revolutionary poses. Down here you could believe the Soviet Union was indeed a worker's paradise, an image that would shatter immediately upon returning to the reality of the grim world above.

One day as Torsten climbed the stairs to his apartment, he heard a thump followed by a Russian expletive. Apples and potatoes appeared from around the corner and rolled down the stairs towards him. Torsten bent down to get them.

"Hey, leave them alone. Those are mine."

"Of course, I was only picking them up for you."

He looked up to see a young woman in a plain brown dress with shoulder length chestnut hair.

"I'm sorry, I should thank you, not accuse you. My shopping bag broke. I queued two hours to get those."

"I'm Torsten. Pleased to meet you."

"Natalya."

"Let me carry these up for you now that I have them."

"I'm afraid I'm on the top floor."

"You can put them on the table," she said when they got there.

The apartment was even smaller than where Torsten lived, just one room with a bed, table and chairs.

"Let me offer you some tea for your trouble. Sit yourself down while I go make it."

Torsten sat on one of the two dining chairs, the only chairs in the room, while she went along the corridor to the communal kitchen. When she returned they sat without talking, sipping their tea and exchanging a smile or two. It was Torsten who broke the awkward silence.

"Do you live here alone?"

"No, I share it with another woman who teaches at the same school as me."

"Do your family live in Moscow?"

"They did. My father was shot during the war and my mother passed away last year. I have no siblings."

"I'm sorry."

"And you. Where did you get a name like Torsten?"

"I was born in Germany." He spoke the word softly as if it was forbidden, expecting her friendly demeanour to change but it didn't. "I was captured, became a Soviet citizen. I'm a deputy at the factory where I work."

"Ah."

"Well, I must be going. Thank you for the tea."
"My pleasure. And thank you for catching my food."
That night Torsten lay in bed thinking of her. Those hazel eyes that seemed vulnerable yet determined, her wistful smile, those prominent cheekbones. His heart beat a little faster.
For the next few days he hung around by the entrance often, hoping to bump into her. As that tactic produced no sighting, he finally plucked up the courage to go and see her. Torsten ran up the steps two by two and then wished he hadn't as his breathlessness made his voice, which already revealed his nervousness, sound choked and constricted.
"I was wondering if you... er...if you would like to go to the park on Sunday. Go to a cafe maybe."
Her expression of surprise at seeing him standing there didn't change.
"Oh. I don't know."

CHAPTER 20

The following silence seemed like an eternity to Torsten. Should he just turn and leave? He decided to accept the rejection.

"I understand. I'll see you around."

"No, wait. All right, why not."

When they reached the park, it began raining. They crammed into the little cafe and had to stand. Tea was all the cafe had so that is what they drank. There was no food to buy.

"Do you miss Germany?" asked Natalya.

"Sometimes. I had an idyllic childhood living in Bavaria, right next to the Alps. But things all changed for the worse when Hitler seized power. Even though the war is over, I can't imagine it will ever be like it once was. I am happy here. I have a job and the Party takes good care of me."

Torsten was circumspect about what he said. A word out of place to the wrong person could have you sent to the gulags in Siberia. Saying what you really thought was dangerous, just as it had been in Nazi Germany.

"Yes, we are lucky to live in a country where everything is provided."

Natalya was equally careful. They didn't know each other well enough to express an opinion on anything political.

"What do you like doing in your free time, Natalya?"

"I love to read the great Russian authors like Gorky, Ostrovsky and Fadeyev. And Tolstoy's War and Peace."

Torsten knew that the first three were government approved writers. Tolstoy's War and Peace had gained acceptance by the authorities for its patriotic story of Russia fighting off Napoleon's invasion. An example for the nation to follow in its struggle against Hitler, even though Tolstoy had been wealthy and not one of the proletariat, which would normally have resulted in an author being banned.

"And I love music. I play the violin. As a little girl I learned ballet. My best childhood memory is going to see the Nutcracker with my parents." Natalya wiped her eyes at the memory. "And you?"

"Once I skied. I was even chosen for the Olympics, but broke my leg and that was that."

"How frustrating that must have been for you."

"It was. Now I enjoy exploring your city. There is much to see."

"There is indeed. Have you been to Gorky Park?"

"No, I haven't."

"Then I shall take you next Sunday."

Soon they had fallen in love and life was bliss. Torsten would sneak up to Natalya's apartment when

Natasha, the teacher she shared it with, was out. After ten years of war, captivity and hard, mundane work, Torsten's world had been transformed into something wonderful by the tenderness he found in Natalya. To touch her was to be transported to a place of ecstasy and abandon.

Her loving soothed away the horrors of the past. Life no longer seemed monotone, there were colours in his mind again. Above all, he felt alive in a way which he hadn't since his childhood. She was the thrill of skiing down a mountain in freshly fallen snow or swimming in a cool lake on a baking hot day all rolled into one. He didn't need to go home, he had found home.

Towards the end of summer, Orlov invited Torsten and Natalya to the dacha outside Moscow which he had use of as a Party official.

It was a splendid late summer day. The chill of early morning had surrendered to a warmth that would itself give way to the colder breath of fast approaching autumn by early evening. The leaves on the silver birches were just beginning to turn from green to yellow as they shimmered in a light breeze like thousands of resting butterflies gathering to fly south.

It was a few kilometres walk from the railway station down a dirt road. Allotments allocated to the privileged few were bursting with late season fruit and vegetables.

The dacha was secluded, hidden by trees and surrounded by flowers. A two-storey wooden building painted green, it blended perfectly with its surroundings.

Orlov and his wife greeted them. An outside table groaned under fresh produce that the young couple could only dream of, and the vodka flowed.

"She's quite lovely," said Orlov as his wife took Natalya for a walk.

"Yes, she is."

"You should take her to the Bolshoi. She would like that. My wife is always dragging me there."

"I'd love to but I doubt I'd get tickets."

"Leave that with me."

Torsten and Natalya returned to Moscow, clutching the jars of jam and pickles pressed upon them by the Orlovs as if they were precious jewels. It had been a truly glorious day, a memory to cherish when the long winter began as soon it would.

Even though most German prisoners of war had now been released and allowed to return home, Torsten thanked his lucky stars that his time in Russia had turned out so well. There was nothing to go back to Germany for. His mother was dead, he had no idea how to contact Ingrid, and if his brother was still alive, he had absolutely no wish to see him.

Torsten often wondered what had happened to Jozef. He fervently hoped that he had lived and enjoyed a good life, but he would never know.

The day that the first snow fell in Moscow that autumn, he was able to surprise Natalya with a trip to the Bolshoi to see Swan Lake. The columns outside and magnificent staircases promised an evening of splendour. Though the hammer and sickle took pride of place and ceiling paintings of Apollo and the muses had been replaced with depictions of peasants, the interior was still largely as it had been in the time of the Tsar.

Red velvet seating and golden decor wowed them both. Despite being up in the very highest balcony, they had an uninterrupted view of the stage.

"Thank you so much for this." Natalya squeezed his hand. "I don't ever remember feeling so happy."

"Me neither."

The stirring but melancholy music of Tchaikovsky caused tears to run down both their faces as they sat completely engrossed in the performance.

As they walked home with thousands of snowflakes whirling around them, Torsten stopped and dropped to one knee.

CHAPTER 21

The wedding was a simple affair. There were no guests and no reception, but the young couple didn't mind. Natalya looked radiant in her white dress, and Torsten considered himself to be the luckiest man alive.

The ceremony took place in one of the state's wedding palaces, albeit it was more like a production line. Tens of couples tied the knot there each day. Afterwards, to demonstrate their good citizenship, they laid Natalya's bouquet by Lenin's Mausoleum in Red Square.

Sergei Orlov sent them a bottle of Soviet champagne and used his influence to get them a new flat. It was the height of luxury. As well as one room to live in, there was a bedroom and a bathroom. And to top it all, he and his wife gave up a weekend at the dacha so the young couple could go in their place.

When Torsten looked back on their trip, he was grateful they had been blessed with such a magical time. They had to wade through the snow as they walked from the station, but once there and with the wood stove going it couldn't have been cosier.

The all enveloping silence was a gift. No neighbours shouting at each other, no echo of footsteps on the stairs, nor the slamming of doors as in Moscow.

In a cupboard, they came across some ice skates which fitted well enough. They went skating on the lake, acting out scenes from Swan Lake and falling about with laughter at their pathetic attempts. On walks in the forest, theirs were the only human footprints although there were many varieties of paw print from small to large, from a wolf or a lynx to a hare or a rabbit.

On one of their outings, the couple came across a cave. Inside, icicles of a blue white hung in their hundreds as if transparent daggers. It was like a scene from a fairy tale, the palace of a wicked witch, and hugely atmospheric.

Torsten discovered a beauty to the Russian winter which he had never imagined existed. It felt as though they were the only two people in the world. A world which was fresh and unsullied. A world of no conflict or oppression. Neither wanted to return to the city.

They fantasised about disappearing into the wilderness, building a log cabin, and living off the land. In summer they would grow vegetables and pick berries, shoot deer and gather wood. They would swim daily in the lake and fish too. Come winter, they would retreat inside and live off what they had stored.

Perhaps they wouldn't be found. However if they were, they would almost certainly be sent to Siberia. Private property was prohibited as was moving without a permit to do so, or being unemployed. Their plans would have to remain unfulfilled.

Moscow closed around them as the train entered the city. The pollution from the capital's power plants hung low in a fog. It was as if a huge cloak of coarse burlap had been thrown over them. But at night in each other's arms, they forgot all that and could pretend that they were in their imaginary cabin. They hoped one day things might change and they would be able to pursue their dream.

Come spring, Torsten was elated when Natalya announced she was pregnant. Early one January morning, their daughter was born. He had never felt such joy as when he first held her in his arms. They named her Olga after Natalya's mother.

Each night, he would rush home from work to be with their baby. Natalya was usually home first, having picked her up from the state creche. Olga would reach out her arms for him and smile. Torsten cuddled and kissed her while Natalya cooked. His life was complete and he was content. The past was the past and the future would be better.

"I need you to do something for me, Comrade," said Orlov some months after the birth. "The Israeli ambassador is coming to visit the factory. We supply them with arms. I won't be here to show him around. I will be at the Party Congress. I want you to take my place. Afterwards, an official car will drive you both out to the dacha to take lunch."

Torsten had read in Pravda, the official newspaper, of the founding of the state of Israel in 1948. The Soviet Union had been one of the first countries to recognise it.

"That sounds exciting," said Natalya as Torsten told her the news when he got home. "And lunch out at the dacha. I'm jealous."

"I'm a little nervous in case he asks me about my past. He'll wonder why I have a German name."

Olga wasn't in the least perturbed at the thought, gurgling with delight as her father jiggled her about on the end of his knee.

"You don't need to tell him you are from Germany. Many people of German descent lived in Russia before the Great Patriotic War."

As the ambassador bent forward to alight from his car, his charcoal coloured hat, which matched his suit, obscured his face. Torsten bowed his head slightly and offered his hand in greeting.

"Delighted to meet you, Your Excellency."

When Torsten looked up, he drew his head back in astonishment. Surely it couldn't be, but it must be unless he had a cousin who looked very much like him. The ambassador smiled briefly. Did he recognise him? If he did, he was giving no indication.

Torsten dutifully showed him around the factory. The ambassador nodded politely, saying little. In the official car they remained silent, each looking forward or out of the window as the chauffeur drove them out into the countryside. Only when they had sat down at the table outside the dacha and the cook had gone back inside, did he acknowledge him.

"Torsten, my dear friend. I never expected to see you. I am so glad you are alive and well."

"And I am so happy to know you are too, Jozef. Never in a million years did I think we'd meet again."

"I know. How did you end up here?"

"After you escaped, I was captured. Eventually, I was assigned to work in the factory. My boss liked my work. He promoted me and got me citizenship. And you, an ambassador. I'm so happy for you."

"Yes, no one was more surprised than me when the Israeli Prime Minister asked me. After you set me free, I went east, and after the war ended I joined other Jews leaving Russia to fight the British in Palestine for a Jewish homeland. Fortunately, Stalin was happy to let us go. I think he believed Israel would in time become a socialist state, which I doubt. He also saw it as an opportunity to undermine British influence in the Middle East. We thought it would take years to achieve our goal, but the British soon threw in the towel and pulled out. Then we had to fight the Arab countries and we succeeded. The Holocaust taught us that meeting force with force is the only way."

"I'm so sorry, Jozef, for what you suffered. So sorry

about your family."
"Me too, but it wasn't your fault. It's not as if you caused their deaths. We can't change the past as much as we'd like to be able to." Torsten looked away. "Is there something the matter, Torsten? You appear troubled."
"There's something you should know. Something I'm very ashamed of."
"What?"
"I...I was the one, who complained about you being picked for the Olympics, being on the ski team. I was jealous, angry that I too hadn't been picked."
Jozef let out a short belly laugh.
"Well, I would never have guessed. But really it doesn't matter. They would have found out anyway. I should thank you. You saved me from months of wasted training. I can't believe that I would ever have been allowed to compete. Can you imagine what would have happened to the team managers if I had won a medal and Hitler had been required to present it to me? How incandescent with rage he would have been?" Jozef closed his eyes briefly recalling the past. "Do you remember those halcyon days when we used to ski, the snow sometimes as soft as flour? Not a care between the two of us, up in the mountains from where the world looked so untroubled."
"Of course I remember. I think about it often."
"Those we're the best of days. Tell me, do you know what happened to your brother?"

"No, he fled before the Russians arrived. I hope he died. He was a monster."

"Indeed he was. My government is trying to track down the worst of those involved in the Holocaust so that they can be brought to justice. Your brother is on the list, though we've had no luck. I expect he's probably dead. So many died unidentified. And you, Torsten, are you married?"

"I am. Natalya is my wife's name and we have a daughter, Olga, who is six months old now. She's the apple of my eye."

"I'm envious. My wife and I are unable to have children. You are blessed. But you deserve to be. Over fifty people escaped thanks to you. People who would have died a most horrible death, lived due to your bravery. And now many are having their own children, bringing new life into this world that is only possible because of what you did. I made enquiries about you. To find out if you survived and where you might be but without success. What a great day this is. It would be lovely to meet your wife. You could come for dinner at the embassy."

"Natalya would love that but I'm not sure we can. We live in a climate of fear and paranoia. The security police probably monitor who comes and goes at the embassy. It would draw attention to us. Stalin rules with an iron fist. Those who give any cause for suspicion are shipped off to labour camps."

"I understand." Jozef stroked his chin, seeking in-

spiration. "I know what. How about if I sent a car to pick you up a few streets away from where you live? The driver will say when you are close, and you can crouch down on the back seats.That way no one would see you enter or leave the embassy."
"Yes, that sounds like it would work."

CHAPTER 22

"I don't think we should take the risk."

"There'll be no risk, Natalya. We merely go out for a walk and a few streets away we get into a car. No one will see us arrive at the embassy. I'd really like to go for old time's sake and for you to meet Jozef."

"OK, I suppose so."

No one else was around the evening they went. Heavy rain had kept indoors those who might otherwise have ventured out. Jozef held an umbrella over them. It not only kept them dry, it also hid their identity. The car was parked on a quiet street. At the embassy, they stepped straight from the car door into the building. Jozef was waiting to greet them

"How wonderful to meet you, Natalya. Your husband is a hero. He saved my life and those of many others. Let me introduce my wife, Sarah."

The diminutive lady at his side in a black and white checked dress and with her dark brown hair swept back into a bun, stepped forward to shake their hands. Her cheeks were full and cherub like. Torsten noticed the tattooed number on her wrist. Like her husband, she too must have suffered terribly.

"I'm so pleased you could come. And who is this little angel?"

"Would you like to hold her?" asked Natalya.

Olga happily went to Sarah, who beamed with joy as she took her into her arms.

Jozef was surprised by how simply furnished the embassy was. He had expected grandeur, plush velvets and large gilded frames holding portraits of national heroes. The decor was modest to the point of being basic. Yet Israel was a new country and a small one, not a great power that had an ego which required stroking with trappings of magnificence.

The men spent much of the evening reminiscing about their boyhood while the women chatted about babies. All too soon it was time to depart.

"I don't know when we'll be able to meet again," said Torsten.

"Before too long I hope, though we are returning to Israel in a few weeks. My time here is almost over. I wish to focus on bringing Holocaust perpetrators to justice. Stalin is over seventy now. His successor may well be more open minded. We may be able to visit you, or perhaps they'll let you come visit us. Who knows? Life has taught me that you never know what can happen, both good and bad. I like to think that the bad is behind us and there is a lot more good still to come."

The journey back to the flat was uneventful. Olga, who had already fallen fast asleep, didn't wake

up when they got out of the car and carried her through the streets and up the stairs to their apartment. After laying her gently in her cot, the couple snuggled up to each other under the sheets.
"See there was no need to worry. I told you it would be fine."
"Yes, you were right. What a lovely couple. I feel for Sarah. Life may not be a bed of roses for us, but we are luckier than them, so lucky to have our baby."
"Indeed we are. And I'm so lucky to have met you."
"And me you. I love you, Torsten. I love you with all my heart."
Two days later, Torsten jumped when he heard the sound. It was years since he had heard that noise. It made his stomach somersault.
He looked out of the living room window. A woman lay face down on the pavement, the contents of her shopping bag were scattered in a pool of blood coming from her head.
"What did you shoot her for? You've killed her," one man reprimanded the other as they stood beside her.
"She ran when I told her to stop."
Others in the street crossed the road and walked on by, heads down. They didn't want to be involved, accused of doing or seeing something they shouldn't.
"We'll have to leave her here for now while we arrest him."
Torsten wanted to run out, run out to his wife.

His legs felt unsteady. He put his hands on the table seeking support and gasping for breath. How could this be happening? But there was no time to think about Natalya at the moment. They had made a solemn promise to each other. More than anything he had to keep that promise.

He grabbed Olga who was crawling around on the floor, and tore down the staircase and out of the rear door. Standing with his back against the wall, he heard them enter the building by the front and go upstairs.

Torsten ran. It wasn't long until he heard them shouting from the open bedroom window. He didn't turn around to look. He had almost reached the cover of another building. Then there was that awful noise again. Expecting the bullet to hit him, he braced himself so as not to fall on Olga. But he didn't. They'd missed.

It wasn't far now. If only he could get there, he'd have a chance.

Reaching the metro, he didn't stop to buy a ticket. In the rush hour crowds, he pushed his way past people, not bothering to apologise.

A train was pulling in. It would only be there a few seconds. If he missed it, they would catch him.

There was shouting behind him now. Looking back for an instant, he saw the two men cursing as they forced their way past commuters.

The doors opened. Torsten reached them and squeezed on. All the time they were getting nearer.

Move. Please move.

The doors shut and the train left. He hugged his daughter tightly. She had begun crying and was asking for Mama. People gave him looks of suspicion and drew away from him, turning their backs on him.

At the next station the train stopped. It stood. Stood for too long. A wave of panic hit Torsten. Had it been ordered to wait? Wait until the secret police got here.

He jumped off. He had never got off at this station before but fate was kind. There was another line here and Torsten changed onto that.

Reaching the stop for the Kremlin, he came back up to the surface. Everything appeared so normal. Trams and government vehicles, and people walking on their way home to their loved ones for a quiet, uneventful evening. A day just like any other. Not how he would have imagined the worst day of his life would be.

Little Olga looked up at him for reassurance. He smiled at her, struggling to hold back the tears welling up in his eyes.

"It's all right darling. We're going on a little trip, an adventure."

Torsten had to make her safe. That was all that mattered now.

Reaching the gate he pressed the bell repeatedly, worried that at any moment he and Olga would be dragged away by anonymous figures.

"You only need to ring once. What do you want?"

said the man arriving at the gate.

"I need to see the ambassador. Now."

"Do you have an appointment?"

"Just open the fucking gate will you. I'm Torsten Drexler, a close friend of his. He'll be extremely annoyed with you if you don't and anything happens to me and my daughter."

Deciding that the wild-eyed man stood before him sounded genuine, the man let him in and led him inside the building.

"Wait here."

Torsten stood in the hallway, swaying Olga back and forth to keep her from bawling.

"Torsten? What are you doing here? Jozef's out right now. He'll be back soon."

Torsten began sobbing and leaned forwards into Sarah's embrace. Once he had calmed a little, she took Olga from his arms and showed him into the room where only a few days earlier they had all sat laughing together.

"Sit down. I'll go get you some tea."

Jozef returned shortly afterwards.

"What will you do?" he asked after Torsten had explained.

"Hand myself into the authorities."

"I feel terrible. This is all my fault."

"No, Jozef, it's not. Don't ever think that. It was my choice. And who knows, maybe it's about something completely different. Something to do with Natalya's school, or me at the factory. Or a neighbour who doesn't like us could have made a false allegation against us. They take people in for the smallest of reasons and sometimes for none at all."

"I will contact the Foreign Ministry and put in a good word for you."

"If you want. I don't really care what happens to me now. I just want Olga to be all right, for her to have a normal childhood. That's why I came here. Natalya and I had discussed what we should do if something like this ever happened to us. We made the other promise to do whatever it took to ensure Olga was safe. I need you to do me a huge favour."

"Of course, whatever I can."

"I want you and Sarah to take care of her. Take her back to Israel when you go."

Both Jozef and Sarah looked stunned.

"Please. Her life will be awful if she stays here. At best they'll send me to Siberia, to a labour camp. That is no place for a child, and nor is a state orphanage if they decide to keep her. I'm begging you."

Jozef looked at his wife who nodded.

"There's no need to beg. We'll gladly take Olga. It will be our privilege. There'll be no problem to get papers for her from our government, and pretend that she's ours."

"We'll take good care of your baby and love her for you until you're free to come join her," added Sarah. "Try not to worry about her. I swear on my life that I will let no one harm her so long as I live.

You must think about yourself."
"Yes, Torsten. Stay strong. You've faced hardship before and got through it. You will this time too. I know you will."
"Thank you, thank you both. There's no need to tell Olga about me or Natalya. I don't want her to grieve for the loss of her parents. One who she'll never see again, and one who in all likelihood she won't either. I don't want her to live with that sadness. She won't remember this awful day, she's too little."
"Are you sure that's what you want?" asked Sarah.
"It is. It's the best thing for her. I don't want her to suffer that awful ache inside that won't go away, like we have all experienced from the loss of loved ones."
Torsten reached out for his daughter who was still in the arms of Sarah. Olga snuggled closer into Sarah, sucking her thumb. Getting down on his knees in front of the armchair where Sarah sat cuddling her, he kissed his child even though she tried to move her face away.
"Goodbye Olga, Daddy has to go do something. Be a good girl now for Jozef and Sarah."
Perhaps suddenly sensing he might not be coming back, Olga wriggled in Sarah's arms, calling out "Papa, papa" and fighting to be free.
Choking back the tears, Torsten didn't look back though he desperately wanted to. If he stayed any longer, he risked the secret police arriving and demanding that his daughter be handed over to

them as well.

CHAPTER 23

As he walked towards the Lubyanka, the headquarters of the NKVD, the predecessor of the KGB, Torsten felt the invisible but overwhelming weight of despair crushing him. The lights had gone out in his world. Torsten no longer cared whether he lived or died.

The interrogating officer at the Lefortovo prison to where he was transferred, didn't seem to care either. Torsten's face was bloody from repeated punches. He could hardly see out from the swollen flesh which had almost closed his eyes completely.

"I will ask again. What secrets did you pass to the Israelis?"

"None. The ambassador was a friend. Someone I helped escape from the Nazis in the war."

The man brought his face level with Torsten's. It appeared to be red with rage, unless there was blood obscuring Torsten's vision. When the man spoke, Torsten felt the spit of his angry words land on his face.

"Listen you little piece of shit, if you don't confess you'll be executed."

Torsten wished for that and hoped it would be soon, that he wouldn't suffer torture like those whose screams of agony came from nearby rooms. His wife was dead. He was never going to see his little girl again. Death would be a welcome release from the hell which his life had so quickly and unexpectedly become.

But they didn't execute him. Whether due to Jozef speaking to the Foreign Ministry or for some other reason, Torsten would never know. A few days later, he was bundled onto a train and crammed into a goods wagon with tens of others. Cold winds whistled through the gaps in the wooden planks making sleep almost impossible.

Although he couldn't see any of it, Torsten was crossing the entire country. He lost count of how many days they took to reach their destination.

When they were finally let out, he could see the ocean. Never before had he seen the sea, other than in photographs which failed to convey how immense it was. Like a huge sheet of undulating steel, it was the colour of dull silver. The thought of ever being out there in a boat sent a shiver down his spine.

Torsten realised that they must be in Vladivostok at the end of the Trans Siberian railway on Russia's Pacific coast, only a few hundred miles from Japan. Having departed from Europe, he was now in the far east of Asia. To his dismay, his exile wasn't complete. Transferred to a leaking rust bucket of a boat, the prisoners now had to endure a thousand mile sea journey north to Magadan, the arrival point for the most notorious gulags of all. During the voyage, the prisoners were kept below deck in darkness. Food was thrown through hatches from above, their only sight of daylight for several days. The ship pitched and rolled in an alarming manner. An all pervasive stench of vomit from the many who suffered seasickness, filled his nostrils night and day. The experience made the train journey seem almost pleasant in retrospect.

In Moscow, the snow hadn't yet arrived. Here in Siberia, winter already had the land firmly under its iron grip. Despite this Torsten was glad to be back on land and out in fresh air when the ship docked and they were at last let out, blinking rapidly as their eyes re-accustomed themselves to daylight.

For days they were marched through the wilderness to reach their camp. It was situated down a secluded track not far from the road which they had come to finish. Little more than a track itself, this road would, when completed, run for over two thousand kilometres from Magadan on Russia's north east coast to Yakutsk in the interior, and capital of Yakutia. A region the size of India, it contained less than one million inhabitants.

Western Russia had been vast. The enormity and emptiness of Eastern Russia was beyond comprehension. In the west of the country you would come across towns or villages. Here there was nothing. Nothing but forests and mountains, frozen rivers and lakes. It felt like the very ends of the earth. A place from which there could be no return.

The authorities didn't even consider it necessary to put a fence around the camp. A few posts marked its limits within which the prisoners were required to stay. Occasional signs of Zapretnaya Zona, or forbidden zone, had been hammered into the ground.

Running would end in almost certain defeat. The local native population, who herded reindeer, were rewarded handsomely if they found an escapee. If they didn't find you, the elements would kill you sooner or later.

On arrival, Torsten's head was shaved. It brought back memories of his time at the concentration camp. Though now he was the prisoner, not the guard, and while death was a strong possibility it wasn't a certainty as in the Nazi death camps.

Hardened criminals, their bodies covered with tattoos, were used to enforce discipline within the gulag. In return, they received better rations and had a much easier time. In this absurd world murderers were treated better than those who had expressed a thought that was deemed to be counter revolutionary, or had been accused of doing so. Guilt was assumed, proof wasn't required.

Torsten resigned himself to his new life. He had already concluded that he deserved this punishment for the bad things which he had done.

It was he who had insisted on dining with the Messings, ignoring Natalya's concern that they could be putting themselves at risk. Torsten had lived in Russia long enough. He knew the system. One step out of line was all it took. He had sacrificed his wife and lost his daughter with his arrogant complacency, destroyed all he cared about for one dinner, one evening with an old friend.

In better physical condition than most, Torsten had an advantage. Those who arrived weak didn't survive. Food rations depended on work done. If you exceeded your quota you got more, if you didn't you got less.

The work was exhausting, much worse then what had been required of him as a prisoner of war. With only basic tools, such as picks, they were expected to hack out a road from the permafrost. The highway had acquired the name 'The Road of Bones'. The skeletons of those who had died lay where they had fallen, except for the many which were used as part of the foundations.

The hot summers never melted the permanently frozen ground just below the surface. Winters with temperatures falling to fifty below ensured that. And summer brought little comfort after winter's extreme cold. Working in the heat was even more debilitating. Constant clouds of mosquitoes made Torsten long for winter's return. His body was permanently covered in bites from them and the bedbugs he shared his nights with. Only spring and autumn were vaguely pleasant, and those two seasons were short here.

Torsten was back in the Dark Ages, a world without electricity or running water and of stinking latrines. Their diet consisted mainly of potatoes and black bread, often so hard it could break a tooth unless softened in liquid such as the buckwheat gruel or watery cabbage soup that was served. On good days, a piece of pig fat would be floating in their dinner. Hunger was a constant, a sucking yearning that refused to be ignored. In summer, like the others he would eat berries whenever he came across them and chew on grass and plants to try and assuage the emptiness in the pit of his stomach.

Amongst those in Torsten's hut were two Muscovites, Petya and Sasha, who he became friendly with. If one was having a bad day, the other two would help out to ensure none of them got onto the fatal slippery slope of reduced rations for less work. Those who did, acquired the nickname a 'goner', slowly starving to death.

"I overheard one of the guards saying Stalin's dead," said Sasha one evening as they huddled around a fire which they had been allowed to make with wood gathered from the forest after they finished work.

"About time the evil bastard pegged it," said Petya. The men trusted each other enough to be open with their views. "Maybe the new leader, whoever he is, will let us go."

It wasn't until several days later that the political

commissar summoned the prisoners one evening to announce the news. Despite the bitter cold, he went on for several minutes about the man's achievements, and how the entire country would strive even harder to achieve the Communist Party's goals to honour Stalin's memory. Then he demanded three minutes silence, becoming angry when any of the men moved to try and keep warm. Hope that the dictator's death would see them freed soon faded. The months rolled by and they remained here.

"Torsten, me and Petya have been talking." The three of them were outside enjoying an autumn evening, now that the cooler weather had dealt with the bane of their life, Siberia's voracious mosquitoes. "Stalin dying hasn't changed a damn thing. We've had enough. We're going to make a break for it."

"But where to? It's no good heading south to China. Mao's troops will just hand you back."

"No, we're going where no one would expect. As you know, Petya was in the air force. He can navigate by the stars. We reckon it's only fifteen hundred kilometres to the Bering Strait. Less than two months walking. By the time we get there, the sea should be frozen over. It's less than a hundred kilometres from there to Alaska and freedom. What do you say? Will you come with us?"

"I don't know. The chances of dying are high."

"Maybe, but better that than a lifetime here."

"What if the sea doesn't freeze over? Not all seas

do."

"We'll steal a boat, or build a raft. Think it over and let us know tomorrow."

Torsten tossed and turned that night. What would it matter if he joined them and they failed? How could death be worse than this life. However, something that he couldn't explain held him back.

On the night of their departure after he had hugged them and wished them good luck, he regretted his decision almost as soon as they had disappeared into the darkness. He had missed his opportunity and it was too late. If he left now he might well never find them, and on his own he would certainly be doomed to failure.

Melancholy gnawed at his soul for days, one that plumbed new depths when a week later his two friends were brought back into camp by local reindeer herders. They pocketed the money which they received and left before Sasha and Petya were shot in front of the others, who were forced to stand and watch their summary execution.

Afterwards, they hung their naked bodies from posts tied by wire. They left them there for weeks. The corpses didn't rot in the cold. They soon became covered with icicles like gross caricatures of Jack Frost.

Other than when in winter the Northern Lights occasionally appeared, dancing in the night sky and lifting his spirits, night was the only time when Torsten managed to escape his world of gloom and unlock a door to anything approaching happiness. Lying there in the pitch black, he remembered his childhood in Partenkirchen and married life in Moscow. He thought of his mother and his sister, and of Natalya and Olga. Through the long days of hardship he kept himself going by thinking about how at night he would use his mind as a means of escape from his wretched reality and go back to those all too brief periods when all had seemed right with the world.

Torsten was at least glad that he had entrusted Olga to Jozef and Sarah's care. His daughter would never have survived in the gulag. She probably would have died on the journey here. He hoped she was happy and that her life would be much better than his, one without the scourge of war and hatred.

About a year after his friends' attempted escape, he was told to report immediately to the camp commander's office. Torsten wondered why as he wiped his clammy palms on his dirty clothes. Though why feel anxious? What could possibly happen that would make things even more unpleasant?

CHAPTER 24

"You are to be freed."

Torsten was struck dumb.

"Well, don't just stand there. Go and join the others lining up outside."

There must have been over a hundred of them who shuffled out of the camp and repeated the long walk they had made years ago. They didn't know that back in Moscow, Nikita Khrushchev, the First Secretary of the Communist Party, had denounced Stalin's excesses and that thousands of prisoners, who weren't considered politically subversive, were being released.

Torsten was required to live in the grim town of Magadan. Only founded in the 1930s, it was without beauty of any kind. Row upon row of shoddy Soviet apartment blocks, and no greenery to soften their utter drabness. Yakutsk, the nearest city, was further away than Berlin was from Moscow or London from Rome. He might be out of the gulags, but he was still completely isolated and condemned to live in a place no one would voluntarily choose.

After a year there, Torsten decided to seek permission to return to Moscow. To his surprise, it was granted. Back in the capital, he was initially given a flat to share with three others. Two slept in the living area, two in the bedroom. It was damp and mould peppered the walls like acne, nonetheless it was a whole lot better than Siberia.

Allocated a clerk's job at the Ministry of Foreign Trade, there he remained for over ten years. He never mentioned his time in the gulags. No one did. You never knew who had spent time there and who hadn't. Everyone knew the camps existed, but it was an unspoken knowledge. Talking about them might get you sent there yourself.

Often Torsten wished he could return to Germany. There was nothing to keep him in Russia any longer. However, his desire had to remain a secret. Asking to leave would be seen as a betrayal of the glorious Motherland. Though the new regime might be less evil than Stalin's, it was still austere and unyielding, demanding total adherence to its cause.

Over the years daily life improved for most. Torsten now had his own one room apartment and a television. Ordinary Russians believed they were living in a golden age. Less than twenty five years since Russia had almost been obliterated, their country was no longer vulnerable. Parades of long range missiles and other military hardware through Red Square on May Day and the anniversary of the October Revolution confirmed the country's status as a world superpower.

People took pride in their country's achievements. Yuri Gagarin had become the first man to go into space. State media assured the workers that they were on course to overtake America at some point in the not too distant future, and that capitalism itself was on the verge of collapse.

The majority were content. There were no more famines or mass executions. They had housing, a job, free education, and free healthcare. Their lives were so much better than their parents had experienced.

As he headed to the Metro to go home one evening, for once Torsten had a spring in his step. It had been the same as any other day at work, filling in forms, checking forms, the same old boring routine. The same as any other day until his boss had summoned him.

"I want you to come to Germany with me next week. I need a translator. The one due to have come has appendicitis. He won't be back for weeks. You'll have to do instead."

"Of course. Are we going to Berlin?"

Russia's foreign trade was largely with other communist countries and, because of his language skill, Torsten was mainly involved with paperwork concerning East Germany, a faithful Soviet satellite.

"No, West Germany. Munich. I'll get your visa and passport organised."

Torsten fought to suppress outward manifestation of the surge of excitement which he felt inside. His boss might change his mind if he detected any hint of it.

Two impassive and unfathomable men from the KGB accompanied Torsten and his boss and the two officials from the Ministry, in case any of them might be tempted to defect.

Torsten got to experience his first ever flight. He gripped the arms of his seat tightly as the engines roared and the jet raced ever faster down the runway at Moscow's Sheremetyevo airport. The angle of climb seemed so steep that he had to fight to stay calm, so convinced was he that the aircraft would fall back to earth and crash.

As the Aeroflot Tupolev 134 descended into Munich, Torsten caught a glimpse of the Alps on the horizon. He wanted to shout out with joy. It had been almost thirty years since he had seen their life affirming outline.

Once in the city they were confined to their two adjacent hotel rooms, emerging only for dinner. Tomorrow, they would meet their supplier in the same hotel and then be driven to the airport for the flight back to Moscow.

Torsten was sharing his room with a work colleague and one of the minders. That man controlled the key, locking them in at bedtime as if they were naughty children.

Light from the street lamps outside penetrated the curtains and defined the shape of objects. Torsten could see it there, on the bedside table. It was tantalisingly close. He wondered if he could do it in time. If he was caught, he'd be bundled on the next flight back and sent off to a gulag again. He was certain of that.

Hoping that it was only him who could hear his galloping heartbeat, Torsten eased himself out of the double bed he was sharing. As he put both his feet on the ground and reached out for the room key, the agent in the bed next to his coughed and turned over in his direction.

Torsten lost his nerve and pretended he was getting up for a pee. For most of the night he lay awake watching, waiting in vain for the minder to turn over again.

All during the meeting the following day, Torsten could barely think of anything else. His chance, his one and only chance was slipping away. When he translated, it was as though he was outside his body, as though it wasn't him talking. Escape was his focus.

However, no opportunity presented itself. At toilet breaks, one of the minders always accompanied him.

Torsten watched the city pass by from the taxi window as they headed out to the airport. Germany must have enjoyed considerable economic success. It looked so prosperous in comparison to Moscow. People thronged the pavements, weighed down with their shopping bags. BMWs and Mercedes clogged the roads, and shop windows displayed goods you'd never see in Russia. Not unless you were one of the privileged few able to shop at stores reserved for the Party elite which sold goods imported from the West.

Even at the traffic lights, Torsten couldn't jump out. A KGB agent sat on one side of him, his boss on the other. Soon they had left the city and were on the autobahn, the prospect of freedom gone. The airport terminal appeared floodlit on the horizon like an apparition.

As they drove up the ramp to departures, he saw the Aeroflot plane, the red flag with its yellow hammer and sickle on its tail, steps already in position waiting for its passengers. Its conical nose and sharp angular lines made it appear more like a military plane than a civilian airliner, and to Torsten it was to be his prison transport back to Russia. In an hour he'd be in there, the door would close. Never again would he get to leave the territory of the USSR.

In the check in line he did it. Suddenly, he made a dash for freedom. The minders came after him.

He weaved around passengers ambling through the hall with their suitcases, bumping into some who shouted at Torsten to look where he was going.

He made it outside. A quick glance behind confirmed he was still being pursued. He ran along the pathway until it was level with the apron and jumped over the low wall.

Tosten was tiring. Almost fifty, he was out of breath. The agents too were over the wall, closing on him. Looking ahead, he realised in his panic

that he'd made a terrible mistake.
Only a few metres away was the Moscow bound plane. He went to run past it but they caught him. In an arm lock, they steered him towards the steps.
Out of the corner of his eyes, he saw two airport workers watching.
"Help me," he yelled in German. "I'm a German citizen. I'm being returned to Russia against my will. Help me."
Springing into action, they hurried over and demanded the minders stop. They didn't. They literally carried Torsten onto the aircraft, his legs kicking uselessly like an animal hanging from an overhead cable at a slaughterhouse. The stewardess at the door didn't look in the least surprised at a passenger arriving in this way, moving aside before closing the door and shutting out the free world.

CHAPTER 25

Torsten was manhandled to the back of the aircraft and seated between the two KGB agents. He could see a couple of police vehicles with their lights flashing approaching the aircraft. The window blind on his row was then shut as were all the others.

There was knocking on the door.

"Police. Open up. We want to talk to the man with you."

The man in the aisle seat next to him walked down the aircraft.

"Tell him this aeroplane is the sovereign territory of the USSR, and the man is a Russian citizen."

The stewardess did so.

"We must talk to him otherwise the aircraft will not be permitted to leave," shouted the policeman from outside.

Torsten could hear the stewardess being told to contact the Aeroflot ground agent who could telephone the Russian embassy for instructions. Noticing him listening, she and the KGB agent moved into the cockpit to continue their conversation.

Several hours passed. No other passengers

boarded. Nobody spoke to him.

Torsten wasn't a religious man but he prayed. Prayed that the aircraft wouldn't be allowed to leave. So long as they remained on the ground there was hope. Every noise from aircraft outside made him tense up. Once those engines started, once this plane moved, his fate would be sealed.

Too wound up to sleep, it must have been past midnight when the minder at the front of the aircraft called for him.

"Come here."

When Torsten got there, the man stood aside then shoved him roughly in the back.

"Go."

The stewardess opened the door. In a state of disbelief, Torsten walked down the steps, shielding his eyes from the bright flashes of reporters' cameras. German officials were waiting for him. One put a blanket around his shoulders as he was led to a vehicle and sped away. They took him to a small hotel on the outskirts of the city.

It was nearly midday when Torsten awoke. Downstairs two men introduced themselves as being from the West German Foreign Ministry. They drove him to an office block where over coffee and strudel they interrogated him.

Torsten's most vivid memory of that afternoon was the aroma and the taste of the coffee. It was an almost sensuous experience after so many years in the Soviet Union. Even when it was available, which was rarely, it was a poor imitation of what was sold in the West.

He had nothing useful to offer in the debrief. Torsten had no access to secrets. His position had been too junior for that. Driven to a scruffy part of town, he was put up in a small flat above a butcher's shop. His accommodation was permeated by the smell of raw meat, but he had lived with worse smells.

"You can stay here for a month while you look for work. Here's some cash for food and stuff. Go to the address on this business card tomorrow to initiate the process of obtaining an identity card. The people there will be able to give you information on finding a job. Goodbye and good luck."

Torsten went out for a walk. The new Germany felt strange. Most of those around him weren't even speaking German. Dark haired, they looked nothing like the Aryan race that Hitler had planned would be the only inhabitants of the Fatherland.

The shop signs were unintelligible to him. He wondered if Jewish people who survived the Holocaust had chosen to return. Surely they wouldn't have wanted to come back to a country that had pursued genocide against them.

When he discovered that these people were Turkish, part of the millions brought over to satisfy the country's labour shortage, he smiled at the irony. How Hitler and his supporters would have been disgusted by the modern nation which had risen from the ashes of defeat.

Torsten's elation at being free gradually gave way to fear. Fear that after so many years he had to take responsibility for himself. In Russia, housing was allocated, jobs were assigned. In the West what happened to him was entirely down to him. Never in his adult life had independent thought been required. Even in the German army he had been directed and controlled.

Finding a job wasn't easy like he thought it would be. Not much more than a decade from retirement age and it was the first time that he had had to apply for one. "Russia you say" became a common refrain at his interviews followed by "We'll get back to you" which they never did, except for the few who bothered to write to say the position had now been filled.

In desperation Torsten took a job as a street cleaner and placed an advertisement in the local newspaper to give private Russian lessons. The lack of take up led him to believe there wasn't much demand for those.

At home in the evenings his thoughts turned to trying to find his sister, Ingrid. All Torsten knew was that she had gone to Berlin before the war and married. He didn't know her new surname. Neither did he have any idea how to go about looking for her.

"You could try the German Red Cross," his supervisor told him when Torsten asked if he had any suggestions for finding lost relatives. "I know one guy who found his brother that way."

"Call us back in three months," said the lady he saw. "We've got so many cases we're dealing with."
He did.
"We haven't been able to start on it yet. Wait another three months and call us then."
One Sunday, Torsten decided to take the train to Garmisch-Partenkirchen. It was early June and the place was picture postcard perfect. He was taken aback by the absolute beauty of its setting. The reality was so much better than his dulled memory had recalled. But as the day progressed, he began to find the allure superficial. Like a mask which hides something that the wearer doesn't want the world to know, there was a darkness here in the sunlight.
The house that came with Gruber's job had become a guest house, but Torsten could still envision the flag that once had flown there, the swastika moving in the wind like a nest of venomous vipers. The Olympic stadium remained and the Nazi architecture of its two towers with embossed Aryan sculptures had survived. The past infected the present.
In shops, on the street, at the cafe where he downed a stein of beer and ate a plate of Wienerschnitzel, Torsten saw them. Faces which he recognised, although they were older, faces which had yelled "Heil Hitler" with such enthusiasm, faces which had shown delight in the light cast by the flames of Kristallnacht. Now they smiled for the tourists who either didn't know or didn't care

about the past.

No one said hello or asked if it was him. Perhaps they didn't remember him, or if they did they were keeping it to themselves. He was an outsider now, but an outsider who knew what had taken place. Maybe they perceived him as a threat to the life which they enjoyed. A witness to what they had been, to what they had believed and so emphatically supported.

He imagined no one here spoke of what had happened. Why would they? An uncomfortable secret they shared but didn't talk about. Torsten also had his secrets, ones which he never talked about.

He wondered if his mother had a grave here. His guess that she hadn't been buried in the churchyard proved correct. Where else she might be, he hadn't a clue.

Curious, he went to the place where everything had started to go wrong, where his innocence had abruptly ended. There was no plaque, no memorial. No trace of what had once stood here.

A new building in chalet style and made of concrete had gone up. The ground floor was a pharmacy, the upper floor probably living accommodation. He doubted its inhabitants knew what had occurred.

Torsten was seized by a sudden need to leave this place, not just here where the Messings had once lived, but the whole town. Despite its chocolate box cover appearance, to him it was where the evil that he'd experienced for so much of his life had first taken root. It could never be the idyll it once had. He hurried to the station, never wanting to return.

When he next rang the Red Cross, they had news.

“We’ve found your sister.”

“Where is she?”

Torsten hoped she wasn’t still in what was now East Germany. What a bitter pill to swallow that would be. Ingrid wouldn’t be allowed to visit him, and he couldn’t go there. There was too great a risk that the authorities would return him to the Soviet Union.

CHAPTER 26

"She lives in Nuremberg and would be delighted to see you."

Excited and nervous in equal measure, Torsten found it difficult to sleep the night before his visit. What would she look like? She had only been a teenager when he'd last seen her. Did he have nephews and nieces? They would probably be grown and have left home by now.

What would he tell her about his life? Natalya, maybe. Olga, no. That was too painful a secret of his to share.

Neither could hold back the tears when she opened the door to her apartment.

"Oh, I'm so happy, Torsten. I thought you were dead."

After they had hugged, she led him to the sofa and sat next to him. They held hands, crying and laughing at the same time.

Torsten took time to observe her. How she had aged, but then so had he. So many years flown by, so many years without each other. Ingrid's hair had turned grey and she had become a close image of their mother.

"Where were you? Why didn't you get in touch sooner?"
"I was captured by the Russians in Poland and taken to Moscow where I lived until last year."
"You poor thing. Was it dreadful?"
"Yes, a lot of the time. But let's not spoil today with that. I'll tell you about it all some day. And you, are you still married? Do you have children?"
"Kurt was killed in the war. We never had any children. When I heard that the Russians were coming I fled from Berlin. I walked west like thousands of others and ended up here. What about you? Do you have any family?"
"No, I married once but it didn't last. I see you have mother's picture on your sideboard along with me and Franz."
"Yes, they are my most treasured possessions. After all what are the other things we collect, just repositories for dust. It's the people who we love that are what's important in life."
"What did mother die of?"
"A stroke. It was for the best that she didn't survive it. The doctors said if she had, she would probably have been confined to a wheelchair and be brain damaged. It's good to remember her for what she was like, not what she would have become if she had lived. If she had been allowed to live that is. As you'll no doubt recall, the Nazis pursued a policy of exterminating the disabled."
"I remember. And Gruber?"
"I don't know. I lost touch with him after Mutti

died. Whether he's still in Partenkirchen, I have no idea, and I don't care. I never liked the man."

"Me neither. If only mother hadn't married him, our lives would have been so different."

"Perhaps, but you and Franz would still have been forced to fight."

"I don't think Franz needed forcing, he worshipped Hitler. Anyway, how about him? Is he still alive?"

Ingrid put her head down, avoiding Torsten's gaze.

"Did he die too?"

"No, but..."

"But what?"

She didn't answer.

"Answer me, Ingrid. I have a right to know."

She raised her head.

"I promised him I wouldn't tell anyone."

"Tell them what?"

"I can't say."

"Come on, Ingrid. He's my brother too." Torsten saw indecision in her eyes. "Well?"

"Yes, you're right. I suppose he wouldn't mind you knowing, you're family, after all. Franz came to see me several years ago. He was living in Italy. He owned a boat repair business. He said people had made false allegations about what he did in the war, that's why he couldn't give me his address."

Torsten absorbed the news.

"That's a shame. I would love to see him again," he lied.

"He thinks you're dead, just like I did. I believe he

might be living by Lake Maggiore. He wrote to me a few times. The postmark was Verbania. I looked it up. It's a town there. I haven't heard from him for several years though. Still, maybe you will find him. He would be so delighted to see you again, his little brother. I'm sure of it. I know you two often fought when you were younger, but as
we grow older I think you come to appreciate how important family is. What else do we have? Do you remember that lovely Christmas we had the year Gruber began renting a room, and Mutti used all the money she had to make it special for us?"

"Yes, it was the best time we ever had. The best Christmas ever. Thinking about it has kept me going many a time when things were tough."

"Do you remember how Mutti told us we must always take care of each other? Maybe if you find Franz, you can help him so he can come home."

"Maybe."

"Anyway, let me get you some coffee, and I have bought some lovely cake from the baker's. I'm afraid I never learned to cook well."

"Did you love Jozef?" Torsten asked while they sat eating.

Ingrid almost choked on her cake.

"Jozef? How did you know about us?"

"I heard you and Mutti talking. Your bedroom was next to mine. Remember?"

"Oh, so you already know that's why they sent me to Berlin. They made me get rid of the baby. I often think about that. Whether it would have been a girl or a boy. The woman who did it, she wouldn't tell me. And whatever she did ended my chances of having children."

"That must have been hard for you."

"It was but which of us has had an easy time?"

"And Jozef, did you love him?"

"I don't know. I was curious about love and sex."

"I was angry when I found out. I wanted to punish him for what he did to you."

"You mustn't blame him. It was my idea, I encouraged him. It wasn't his fault. Sometimes I wonder what happened to Jozef. I can only think he must have died, so many did. What a truly awful time it was."

"Well, I have good news for you there."

"You do?"

"I saw him in Russia. He came to the factory where I worked. He was the Israeli ambassador, can you believe. He came to inspect as we sold arms to Israel. He'd married and had a daughter."

Ingrid placed her arms diagonally across her chest.

"Oh, Torsten, that's such wonderful news. I'm so glad. What a perfect day this is. I get to meet my dear brother again, you may soon see Franz, and I find out that Jozef lived."

CHAPTER 27

The train journey from Munich to Verbania took all day long. The ride across Switzerland, which shares Lake Maggiore with Italy, was glorious. The antithesis of Torsten's mood.

He sat there brooding. Though his eyes saw mountains and meadows, churches and chalets, none of these registered. His brother lived. Torsten didn't have a plan, but somehow he needed to make his brother pay. Pay for everything.

On arrival, he could see straightaway why Verbania would have appealed to Franz. It was like an Italian version of Partenkirchen. Next to the lake, mountain peaks filled the horizon.

The terracotta tiled roofs radiated warmth, a place for the good life. A place to hide in comfort.

After leaving his luggage at a small Pensione a few streets back from the lakeshore, Torsten strolled down to the water. Holidaymakers sat outside enjoying their evening meals. At the far end of the path was a boat repairers. 'Pirozzi' the sign said on a unit painted a pale blue. Motor boats in various stages of disrepair lay around the yard. A high metal fence protected it and the gates were locked.

Torsten returned the following morning. This time the gates were open. If this wasn't the correct spot, they would surely be able to tell him of any other boat repairers in town.

"Sprechen Sie Deutsch?" he asked a man painting a boat.

"A little."

"Can you tell me who the owner is?"

"Signor Fischer."

Torsten's heart quickened. A German name.

"Is he in the office?"

"No, he's not here today. He's at home."

"Oh."

"See that large pink villa up there in the hills. That's where he lives. Very nice, eh?"

"Indeed. Thank you. Ciao."

Torsten got the taxi to drop him off before they reached the villa. From up here, there were commanding views of the town and lake below. Motor boats left white trails in their wake on the enticing blue waters. Up on these slopes all looked right with the world, just as Partenkrichen had from the summit of the Zugspitze. Here the past could be forgotten, consigned to history. Exactly as Franz would have wanted.

The house stood behind railings and closed gates and there were bars at the windows.

Torsten walked by, not wanting to draw attention to himself. Sunk in the large patio out front was a swimming pool. A man was in there doing his morning exercise. Turning around and coming back, Torsten dipped behind some bushes on the other side of the road and crouched down to wait. The man got out. He had his back to him. After towelling himself dry and grabbing a pair of sunglasses, he went over to a lounger which faced the house.

Torsten got only a sideways glimpse. The man had a large middle-aged paunch. It could well be his brother. He had the same swagger, the same hair colour, and was the same height, but Torsten couldn't be completely sure.

When the man got up and went into the villa Torsten departed, walking down the steep road back to Verbania. He didn't know what to do next.

Rounding the last bend, he had an idea. Once back in Munich, he rang directory enquiries.

"The Israeli Embassy in Bonn, please."

That small provincial town by the banks of the Rhine had become the capital of West Germany when Germany had been split into two.

Torsten dialled the number they gave him.

"Hello, I have some information for Jozef Messing, who used to be your ambassador to Russia, about a Nazi war criminal. I think I may have found him."

"Hold on please. Let me put you through to someone who can help."

"You can give me the information," said the man who took his call.

"No, I wish to speak to Jozef. I'll leave you my number. You can tell him my name is Torsten

Drexler, an old friend. Goodbye."
The next evening his telephone rang.
"Torsten?"
"Is that Jozef?"
"Yes. How are you, and how did you manage to get out of Russia?"
"I'll tell you sometime. Listen, I think I've found Franz. I can't be a hundred per cent sure, but I'm almost certain."
"No problem. We'll check it out. Where is he?"
"What would you do if you found him?"
"Take him back to Israel for trial."
"I don't want him executed. I want him imprisoned so that he can know what it's like to spend life in a cage, trapped and unable to leave so he can reflect on what he's done."
"I'd need to clear that with the responsible government minister. I'll call you back soon."
Only ten minutes later Jozef phoned him back.
"He's agreed. No death penalty would be sought, only life imprisonment."
"Good. He's in Italy. But I want to be there when you confront him. Can you come to Lake Maggiore?"
"Of course. I'd go anywhere in the world to bring him to justice. When were you thinking of?"
"How about Saturday?"
"I don't know...actually, yes, I'll be there. It's worth interrupting the Sabbath for this."
Torsten and Jozef hugged when they met in the shadowy recesses at the back of a restaurant down

by the lake. The other diners were eating al fresco enjoying the sunshine. The two friends
laughed that they each now had severely receding hairlines.

"My sister told me he might be here. As I said on the phone, I can't be absolutely positive, but there's a man going by the name of Fischer, who lives up in the hills. I'll show you where."

"My men will go check it out and report back to us."

"Then what?"

"If it is him, we'll go in tonight. There's an El Al plane waiting at the airport in Milan. By morning, he'll be in Tel Aviv."

CHAPTER 28

"I still want to be there when you go in."

"You will be. You have my word."

Torsten explained about the boatyard and the location of the villa. Jozef disappeared briefly to talk to his men.

"Why don't we go and sit outside now. It's so dismal back here," he said when he returned.

They sat enjoying the warm weather as they drank a glass of Soave and waited. It seemed odd to think that as the tourists around them chatted and laughed, only up the road from them a mass murderer who had evaded justice for over twenty years could finally be about to face it.

Torsten told Jozef of his life since they had last seen each other.

"I'm so glad you made it out and back to Germany. But you haven't once asked about Olga."

"I'm afraid to. She isn't mine anymore."

"She'll always be yours. Yours and Natalya's."

Torsten rubbed his eyes to try and disguise the tears which had formed.

"Olga's a beautiful young woman now and has done outstandingly well at school. She wants to study medicine. You'd be very proud of her. She'll be eighteen in a few months."

"I know."

"Sarah and I were planning on telling her about her true parents. She'll be an adult."

"No, I don't want her having the pain."

"But why? You're still alive. She could meet you, visit you."

"I would like to meet her, but I don't want her to know who I am. It might sound strange but that's all I need," said Torsten.

"But what about Olga?"

"She's happy now I take it?"

"Yes, very much so."

"Good. I don't need that to be upset by the past."

Jozef sighed.

"It seems a shame for her not to know what a wonderful man her father is. I am going to propose to my government that you are honoured as one of the Righteous Among the Nations. It is a recognition of non-Jews who helped us during the Holocaust."

"I hardly think I deserve it."

"You most certainly do, and I'm sure my government will agree. I hope you will come to Israel to receive the honour in person."

"Perhaps. Jozef, there's something I should have told you years ago. About Ingrid. She fell pregnant. They sent her off to Berlin and made her get rid of the baby. Your baby."

"Oh." Jozef bit his lip.

"I was angry with you for a long time when I found out. I blamed you. When I saw Ingrid recently, she told me it wasn't your fault, that it was her idea."

"I often wondered what had happened, never hearing from her again. I thought she must have decided to end things between us. It was understandable. How could she have married a Jew? But a child. I am sad they killed it. Sad for Ingrid. I have been fortunate to have Olga to take care of. Poor Ingrid, that must have been so terrible for her."

"I believe it was. She never had any other children."

"I'm sorry to hear that. She would have made a wonderful mother."

A car pulled up opposite.

"Look, your men are back."

The two friends walked across the street and got into the vehicle. Jozef spoke to the men inside in Hebrew. Torsten waited for Jozef to translate, keen to know the outcome.

"It's definitely Franz. We'll take you back to your hotel and pick you up after dark."

Torsten's nerves were frayed when they arrived. At last, after all these years he would get to meet his brother once more. Though his brother would be the vulnerable one this time, Torsten couldn't shake off his apprehension. Franz was his nemesis, the physical embodiment of all that had intimidated him as a youth, something he'd never really got over. Maybe this final meeting would end all that, finally free him from his past.

They parked half a kilometre from the villa. It was in complete darkness.

The three armed Mossad agents went ahead. Cutting the lock on the gates, they signalled at Jozef and Torsten to follow. All five of them wore black balaclavas with holes for their mouths and eyes only. An agent picked the lock to the front door and beckoned to them to follow.

Inside a door opened and then quickly shut. They pushed at it, forcing their way in. A woman screamed. Someone hit the light switch.

Franz stood there naked, his mouth open in horror and disbelief. The young woman in his bed pulled the duvet up under her chin.

"Take what you want. Just don't hurt us."

"Get dressed, Franz Drexler," said Jozef.

"I'm Johann Fischer. You've got the wrong man."

"No, we haven't. You may have aged Drexler, but I'd recognise that face anywhere, and that voice. For over twenty years, they've given me nightmares but not any more. Finally, you're going to be held accountable for your crimes against humanity. Now put some clothes on or do I have to shoot you."

Franz almost fell over in his haste to pull his trousers on.

"Tie her up and gag her. We don't want any more screaming," Jozef said to one of the agents. "Take us to the living room."

"You're making a terrible mistake," said Jozef as he complied.

Jozef ignored his comment
"Put that lamp on and sit down there."
Franz was beginning to recover from the initial shock.
"Who are you?"
Jozef pushed back the sleeve of his black long-sleeved t-shirt and thrust his lower arm towards Franz's face.
"Does that answer your question?"
In the dim light, Torsten could make out the numbers tattooed on Jozef's skin. Branded like cattle, a daily reminder for those who bore one of the atrocities which had been perpetrated against defenceless millions.
"I was acting under orders, I had no choice," pleaded Franz.
"I don't think so. You relished all that you did. I watched you. Shooting people on the spot for the most trivial of things. You enjoyed it, never gave it a second thought. I saw the look of satisfaction in your eyes as thousands were marched into the gas chambers."
"Hello, brother." Torsten had removed his balaclava. Once more, Franz was taken by complete surprise. "Bet you never thought you'd see me again."
"You? What are you doing here? Did you bring them here? How could you!" His anger had overcome his fear. "I should have shot you that day when I had the chance."
Jozef removed his mask too, but Franz showed no

sign of recognition.

"You don't even know who I am, do you? I'm just another filthy Jew in your eyes."

"It's Jozef Messing, Franz," said Torsten.

"Messing...Oh, I remember. The shoemaker. You let yourself be brainwashed by the Jews and their propaganda. But I don't suppose you've shared your little secret with him?"

"I already know about the ski team for the Olympics, Drexler. It doesn't matter. Torsten didn't kill, not like you."

"Is that what he told you."

CHAPTER 29

"Yes, he fought in the army. He had to or he would have been shot. But he freed so many from your camp, people you would have murdered in a heartbeat."

"Hmm." There was an arrogance in Franz's manner now. The years hadn't changed him. "My dear brother must have omitted to tell you about what happened on Kristallnacht, the night your family died."

"No, he's told me. He was in the crowd. What choice did he have? You and Gruber dragged him along."

"Yes, we did. In Partenkirchen. We'd finished, we were ready to go home. Then a little voice spoke up. What about the Messings in Garmisch someone said. That was you, wasn't it, Torsten."

Torsten didn't answer. "What? Did you think I wouldn't notice it was you, hiding at the back like the coward you are?"

Bewildered, Jozef looked at his friend. Torsten said nothing but his facial expression pronounced his guilt.

"Torsten? Tell me it's not true."

"I can't, Jozef. I'm so sorry. I was trying to impress the others. Prove myself to be reliable, a good Nazi. I thought they would just drive you and your family out of town. I never imagined that they'd set fire to your home."

Jozef turned to the agents.

"Take him out to the car. I'll be out in a while. I'll deal with the woman when I leave."

Franz gave Torsten a supercilious smile as they led him away.

Jozef slumped into an armchair and lowered his head into his hands.

"I can't believe this. How could you?"

"I was just a stupid teenager. Things got out of control. But yes, it was my fault."

"And you hid it from me all these years? How could you live with yourself?"

Torsten had no words. He couldn't defend the indefensible.

Jozef closed his eyes and pursed his lips as he flung his head back onto the chair. The silence was long and angry. A gaping chasm had opened up between them.

After a short time, Jozef got up and went to the bedroom to take off the woman's gag. As he passed the living room on his way out, Jozef stopped in the doorway and gave Torsten a withering look.

"As for you, you can walk back to town. You're right, your daughter shouldn't know who her father is."

Torsten heard the car drive away and a soft sobbing coming from the bedroom.

CHAPTER 30

On the long train journey back, Torsten watched rain droplets run down the window. Strange as it might seem he was relieved the truth had finally come out, relieved that the secret which he had carried inside of him for so many years was no longer a secret. What he'd done had been wrong, and keeping it from Jozef had been wrong also. He'd lived a lie for far too long.

Perhaps what he'd done so thoughtlessly on that November evening thirty years ago had effected his whole life. Were the years in a POW camp, those years in the gulag, losing his wife and his daughter, all punishment for that one terrible night? Those few careless words. If only he had kept his mouth shut.

Did he deserve to suffer for the rest of his life? Torsten wouldn't get to be the judge of that. Fate or God would determine what happened to him.

Ingrid called him a few days later, her voice constricted with emotion.

"Did you see the news about Franz? He's been kidnapped and taken to Israel. He'll never get a fair trial there. You didn't tell anyone what I'd told

you, did you?"
"I went to Verbania to see if it was him. And yes, I reported his whereabouts. Our brother was a monster. He murdered so many innocent people."
"That's lies, just Israeli propaganda. How could you, Torsten? You've betrayed me, and Franz. Please don't ever contact me again."
Ingrid put the phone down. Once more Torsten was truly alone in the world.
He followed the trial of his brother in the newspapers. Witnesses went to Israel from all over the world to give evidence. What Torsten had seen his brother do was only the tip of the iceberg. It became clear that his sadism had known no bounds.
Franz showed no remorse. When sentenced to life, he shouted out that they had all deserved what they got, and that Hitler had been right all along. He had to be dragged out of the court room as he gave the Nazi salute and refused to move.
Torsten wondered if he also should have been prosecuted. He'd helped cause deaths. Not intentionally, but what he'd started had ended four innocent lives.
His life seemed pointless without family or friends. Perhaps that was to be his final punishment, to live out the rest of his days unknown and unloved.
A loud silence became the soundtrack to his life. He may have worked in the noisy city streets amongst the crowds but they didn't notice him as they passed. Nobody spoke to him.

Torsten was that anonymous street cleaner, probably eccentric, maybe a little unhinged and best avoided. When he occasionally tried to make eye contact with passers by, they invariably looked the other way. Without realising, he had built a wall of unapproachability around himself.

At times when he was feeling particularly low, Torsten thought about ending it all. He could no longer visualise Natalya or Olga. He possessed no mementoes, not even a solitary photograph of either. Their faces had faded until all he could see were heads without any features, as if they were blank masks with only holes for eyes. It was as if they had never existed, as though they had only ever been nothing more than a dream. One that he couldn't properly remember when he awoke, though he tried so very hard to.

However, something always stopped him killing himself, although Torsten wasn't always sure why. He didn't believe it was fear. His life had brought him a great deal of that. So much in fact that fear no longer had a hold over him the way it did over other people who had led more ordinary lives. Maybe it was the memory of his father and what he had done. Yet who would suffer if Torsten did the same? He wouldn't be leaving behind a wife and children. No one would shed a tear or be forced to carry his coffin under the judgmental gaze of others.

A black cat with white paws was sitting outside his door one day when he reached his third floor apartment. Torsten took pity on her plaintive miaowing and fed her. He asked around but none of his neighbours knew where she came from so he kept her. In the evenings, she sat on his knee and at night slept on his bed. She was his only companion.

His life was bleak, not only in the winter months of grey skies and freezing fogs but in summer too. When not working, he never went out. On sunny days, he kept the blinds shut. Sunshine made him feel lonelier than darkness. Too many people were out there enjoying the weather with friends and family, things which he would never have, something which he didn't want to be reminded of. He felt more alone on the crowded streets or in a park than he did shut up in his apartment.

Several months after Franz had been convicted, he got home from work to find a letter from Israel. He had no idea why his brother would write to him. Torsten opened the envelope expecting to be faced with a diatribe of hatred.

Dear Torsten,

In my life I have had many shocks, but hearing of what you did was perhaps the greatest shock of all.

I have experienced the full gamut of emotions since then. Rage, hatred, sadness. None of them have brought me peace or closure.

I accept that what you did, you did in the heat of the moment in no way intending the awful consequences which followed. And even if it were possible to rewind the clock and undo things, my family and I would most

probably have died a horrible death in a concentration camp. Our fate was already sealed, regardless of what you said that night.
The revenge of never letting you see Olga brings me no satisfaction. It punishes her too.
I do believe that you are truly sorry for what you did, and you did save my life and the life of many others at great risk to yourself. You also gave Sarah and I the greatest joy of our lives by entrusting Olga to our care. She has been our shining light.
We all make mistakes. I know I have, like persuading you and Natalya to come to the embassy in Moscow. Something which I will regret until my dying day.
I have therefore decided that it is right to forgive you. Sarah and I are taking Olga to Paris next month as a belated birthday gift. We shall be staying at the Hotel Le Bristol, rue du Faubourg St. Honoré. If you would like to meet your daughter, come there at 5pm on the 25th and meet me in the lobby. We would be glad to see you.
Jozef
Torsten sat down, holding the letter in his shaking hands. He too was shocked. Never did he think that he would hear from Jozef again. Ashamed and humbled, he began to cry. The tears spilled out of him, a dam of regrets bursting. Only when after a while the cat jumped up on his lap and purred did he stop.
When he arrived at the hotel, Torsten was in a state of high anxiety. He had changed his mind so many times about whether this was the right

thing to do. Entering the lobby, he took off his sunglasses. Jozef was waiting and came over.

"You decided to come. I'd been starting to think that you wouldn't."

"I almost didn't. Thank you for this, Jozef. You don't know how much I regret that night. If I could change but one thing in my life, that would be it."

"We're all conditioned by our upbringing, Torsten. If you had been born me and I you, how can I be sure that I wouldn't have done the same? You've suffered enough. We've all suffered enough. Let's talk no more of the past. Come, they're outside."

His heart racing, Torsten followed Jozef into the bright sunshine.

A young woman was sitting with Sarah at a table beneath a large umbrella. She stood up as they approached and walked towards them.

Torsten's mouth became dry. He swallowed hard and felt himself trembling. Inexplicably, those forgotten memories came flooding back to him as though it were only yesterday. It was as if Natalya had come back from the dead. That smile, those eyes, the colour of her hair, they were her mother's. His wife lived, she lived in their daughter.

"Hello, father. Papa told me all about how you saved my life and his. I'm so happy that you came. I feel very lucky to have three parents."

She gave him a kiss on the cheek and hugged him.

ALSO BY DAVID CANFORD

Betrayal in Venice

Sent to Venice on a secret mission against the Nazis, a soldier finds his life unexpectedly altered when he saves a young woman at the end of World War Two. Discovering the truth many years later, Glen Butler's reaction to it betrays the one he loves most.

Kurt's War

Kurt is an English evacuee with a difference. His father is a Nazi. As Kurt grows into an adult and is forced to pretend that he is someone he isn't for his own protection, will he survive in the hostile world in which he must live? And with his enemies closing in, will anyone believe who he really is?

A Heart Left Behind

New Yorker, Orla, finds herself trapped in a web of secret love, blackmail and espionage in the build up to WWII. Moving to Berlin in the hope of escaping her past, she is forced to undertake a task that will cost not only her life but also her son's if she fails.

The Throwback

A baby's birth on a South Carolina plantation threatens to cause a scandal, but the funeral of mother and child seems to ensure that the truth will never be known. A family saga of hatred, revenge, forbidden love, overcoming hardship and helping others.

Sweet Bitter Freedom

The enthralling sequel to The Throwback.

Going Big or Small

A Man Called Ove meets Thelma and Louise. British humour collides with European culture when retiree, Frank, gets more adventure than he bargained for when he sets off across 1980s Europe hoping to shake up his mundane life. Falling in love with a woman and Italy has unexpected consequences.

Bound Bayou

A young teacher from England achieves a dream when he gets the chance to work for a year in the United States, but 1950s Mississippi is not the America he has seen on the movie screens at home. When his independent spirit collides with the rules of life in the Deep South, he sets off a chain of events which he can't control.

When the Water Runs out

Will water shortage result in the USA invading Canada? One person can stop a war if he isn't killed first, but is he a hero or a traitor? When two very different worlds collide, the outcome is on a knife-edge.

2045 The Last Resort

In 2045, those who lost their jobs to robots are taken care of in resorts where life is an endless vacation. For those still in work, the American dream has never been better. But is all quite as perfect as it seems?

Sea Snakes and Cannibals

A travelogue of visits to islands around the world, including remote Fijian islands, Corsica, islands in the Sea of Cortez, Mexico, and the Greek islands.

SIGN UP

Don't forget to sign up to receive David Canford's email newsletter including information on new releases and promotions and claim your free ebook

ABOUT THE AUTHOR

David started writing stories for his grandmother as a young boy. They usually involved someone being eaten by a monster of the deep, with his grandmother often the hapless victim.

Years later as chair lady of her local Women's Institute, David's account of spending three days on a Greyhound bus crossing the United States from the west coast to the east coast apparently saved the day when the speaker she had booked didn't show up.

David's life got busy after university and he stopped writing until the bug got him again recently.

As an indie author himself, David likes discovering the wealth of great talent which is now so easily accessible. A keen traveller, he can find a book on travel particularly hard to resist.

He enjoys writing about both the past and what might happen to us in the future.

Cambridge University educated, his previous jobs include working as a mover in Canada and a sandblaster in the Rolls Royce aircraft engine factory.

David works as a lawyer during the day. He has three daughters and lives on the south coast of England with his wife and their dog.

A lover of both the great outdoors and the man-made world, he is equally happy kayaking, hiking a trail or wandering around a city absorbing its culture.

You can contact him by visiting his website at DavidCanford.com

Made in the USA
Las Vegas, NV
02 February 2021